BIRTHRIGHT BAY

BIRTHRIGHT BAY

a novel by

RUSS POMMER

BIRTHRIGHT BAY
is an imprint of
FLYBYWIRE IMPRINTS
Naples, FL

PALMETTO
P U B L I S H I N G
Charleston, SC
www.PalmettoPublishing.com

Copyright © 2024 by Russell E. Pommer

Paperback ISBN: 979-8-9906490-0-2
ebook ISBN: 979-8-9906490-1-9

LCCN: 2024915904
Copyright Registration Number - TXu 2-412-989

In fond memory of
my friend and colleague
ADAM R. KOKAS

CHAPTER ONE

To echo Herman Melville's famed words, *call me Ishmael.* That has been my name since I was six months old, when my parents, Edgar and Joan Dreyer, adopted me through Louise Wise Services, a Jewish adoption agency in New York City, and selected Ishmael Dryer as my legal appellation. Before that, my name was Michael.

Growing up, I wasn't keen on the name Ishmael but never thought to ask my parents how in the world they came up with it. Perhaps it emanated directly from Melville, as my father considered himself erudite and talked a lot about the literary masterpieces he had read as a kid, including Herman Melville's epic *Moby-Dick*, the poem "If" by Rudyard Kipling, and the novels *Kidnapped* and *Treasure Island* by Robert Louis Stevenson. Growing up, my mother had taught Sunday school at her synagogue (that was before her rejection of Judaism as too in-your-face culturally, to the horror of her childhood friends), so perhaps my name held biblical appeal. I certainly prefer Ishmael to Rudyard (for Kipling) or Ichabod, from Washington Irving's short story "The Legend of Sleepy Hollow," another of my father's favorites.

As I was thinking about this not long ago, a light bulb in my head started blinking. Hardly a biblical scholar, I discovered that in the Old Testament Ishmael was an outcast, banished by Abraham (along with Hagar, Ishmael's mother) after Sarah gave birth to Isaac, who then became Abraham's designated heir. Could my parents have selected the name Ishmael because they thought of me as an outcast, which I suppose I was in the literal sense? I strongly doubt it. Or perhaps the name Ishmael embodied their desire to save me from growing up as a societal outcast in an orphanage. Under that postulate, my parents would have whisked me away from one extreme (being a castaway) directly to another (living in a loving home). Those possibilities, of course, are theoretical. I do not know why my parents chose my name.

What I know with certainty is that my parents loved me to a fault and created the idyllic environment intended by Louise Wise Services. When I was four, we moved from a one-bedroom apartment in Jackson Heights, Queens, to a new split-level in a Long Island bedroom community. I had a large yard and woods in which to play, a maze of streets through which to ride my bike, and eventually, a Dalmatian we called Puppy. She was named after the poor dog my parents had had during the war, who died after eating rat poison that a neighbor had placed in his yard. When I was six, my parents decided to buy a small sailboat, which they named Lady Joan. I learned to sail and acquired a lifelong love of the water and everything nautical. Years later, I learned from my grandmother that, when I was three or four years old, my parents had planned to adopt another child, a girl they planned to name Susan. However, they backed out after I asked if we could return her if we didn't like her.

I was a nervous kid, and my parents were happy to provide the protective shell it felt calming to visualize. Having assessed my upbringing, I now think they also seemed overly protective. When I was six or seven, I slid off the bow of our sailboat into the water. Even though I had a life jacket on and knew how to swim, my father immediately jumped into the water to save me. I was fine, but my mother was not because she didn't know how to sail. The boat was moving in circles on its own, and my mother was screaming as she tried to control it. Fortunately, my father was able to grab hold of the boat and climb on board, saving the day. I followed him on board, happy to have had the new experience.

My friends called me Ishmael because my parents always used my full name. I never imagined I could have a nickname. In eighth grade, I had a truly cool English teacher named Mr. Cornell, who was only in his late twenties but seemed extremely sophisticated. Mr. Cornell had a light blue Corvette convertible, which, reportedly, his father had bought for him so he could establish himself as a chick magnet. Rumor had it that he was dating a high school girl who lived in my neighborhood. I am not certain that was accurate, but I do know for a fact that the two of them married several years later. Mr. Cornell changed my life by lightheartedly calling me "Ish," "Little Ish Dreyer," sometimes "Ish the Knish," and occasionally "Itch," which I thought was especially funny. I started to call myself "Ish" whenever I could. The nickname stuck, in school at least. It felt liberating.

I always knew that I was adopted, and that Louise Wise Services was my adoption agency, but I never felt comfortable talking about it at home. Presumably, someone from Louise Wise did at least one home visit early on, but I have no memory of that. My parents never talked about the process with me or told me why they had adopted a child. I guessed my mother had been unable to conceive and that my birth mother had gotten pregnant out of wedlock and been too young to keep me. I was not certain because the unspoken premise at home was that asking questions would show a lack of love and respect for my parents.

I never thought about, or fully appreciated, the commitment my parents made to me by paying for 100 percent of my higher education. They could have insisted that I earn and contribute money for expenses, but that was not once a topic of conversation. I did well in school, went to college in northwestern Massachusetts, and graduated from law school in Boston. Getting a law degree seemed like a smart option and elegant choice for someone like me who had no real clue what to do in life. I figured eventually I would have an "aha" moment, when lights would begin to flash, revealing my life's true calling. My parents wanted me to return to New York, work in a top-tier law firm, and marry the girl of *their* dreams. Instead, I stayed in Boston, found a job at a firm specializing in maritime law, and married Rachel, whom I had met on the Eastern Airlines Shuttle. Rachel had strong ideas about a great many matters and challenged my parents' belief that a daughter-in-law should be respectful and compliant. During the early years of our marriage, I tried to shoulder the role of peacemaker.

This was my first abject failure. I should have known it would be such because, as before, my parents tried to set the rules and expected Rachel to comply. They wanted me to compel Rachel to be a "good wife" by bending to their will. *It would never happen,* I knew. As the pressure from my parents mounted, I felt as though I were stuck in the formidable maze of hedges at England's Hampton Court, with no ability to escape.

That, fortunately, was a long time ago. After my parents died, a family friend told me that my bad memories would eventually fade, leaving me to remember only the good times. That did not happen, but I did figure out strategies to avoid looking back and instead to move forward.

During the good years, I heard multiple stories about relatives on both sides of the family. I listened politely and never had an overarching desire to pursue them. I knew that my parents were both New Yorkers, with my mother having grown up in Queens and my father on the Upper West Side of Manhattan. Probably the most disquieting fact was that my father's parents refused to attend my parents' wedding because my mother was not of high enough social status. I was not particularly interested in the information that my mother's father had grown up in Savannah, Georgia, where there had been a robust Jewish community since the 1600s, or that my mother's mother had to flee her San Francisco childhood home, along with the rest of her family, during the 1906 earthquake. I took in the information but never considered what it must have been like for my maternal grandfather's own grandfather to be a drummer in the Confederate army during the Civil War. Even my father's service in England as a B-17 navigator in the Eighth Air Force during World War II seemed unremarkable. He won both the Air Medal and the Distinguished Flying Cross for flying into Germany but kept them under his pile of white handkerchiefs in his top dresser drawer. Like many World War II veterans, my father never wanted to talk about the war.

I was as close to my parents as they were to me, but we were never especially close to my living relatives. My father's mother's sister, Tess, ten years older than his mother, was a working woman in the 1950s and early 1960s, with a high-level position at Emerson Radio Corp. That fact alone made her stand out from many other women who, like my grandmother, seemed content in their housewife roles. A stout woman, Tess lived out of wedlock with her gentleman friend, Mort, a man twenty years her junior. Together they owned a twenty-acre farm in New Jersey, where they rode horses, boarded their Dalmatians, and grew vegetables. When I was a small kid, a preteen, and eventually a teenager, that seemed idyllic to me. Occasionally we drove to New Jersey so I could ride the horses, which I loved. We regularly spent holidays with my mother's brother and his family at our house or theirs on Long Island. These were not fun times, notable mostly for raised voices between my father and my uncle about things neither should have been so passionate about. Because my uncle changed jobs frequently, my father thought he lacked the requisite commitment to provide for his family. My uncle thought my father was boorish and stuck-up. Watching them verbally spar over the holiday turkey afforded me a valuable lesson. I realized that no matter what epithets you call another person or how loudly you speak, you are not going to change someone else's mind. That led to my belief that it is better to listen to the views of other people and respectfully disagree than to flog others with epithets until they relent.

CHAPTER TWO

As I would learn years later, Artem Finberg was born in February 1930 into a typical Jewish family in the East Flatbush section of Brooklyn. He had three older brothers, the eldest of whom had been born in Ukraine before their parents, Leonard and Iryna, emigrated in 1924. Perhaps because of the age difference, Artem was not close to any of his brothers. The house in which they lived was not large or grand, but it was all the family needed. Leonard worked as a cutter in the garment business, and Iryna was the consummate homemaker, making blintzes and baking rugelach for the family each week. As a kid, Artem especially loved to play stickball in the neighborhood. After many games, he and his friends would congregate at Rosie's Diner on Remsen Avenue, munching on french fries, slurping on black-and-white shakes, and whistling at the cute girls who regularly walked by.

A tough kid with street smarts, Artem also had brains. His brothers were smart enough to attend Townsend Harris High School, a New York public school for "gifted" students that fed into the City College of New York. It was almost ordained that Artem would attend Townsend Harris like his brothers, but in 1942 Mayor La Guardia closed the school. Although the mayor cited budgetary reasons, Iryna thought something more nefarious was going on and vowed never to vote for another Republican. Throughout her life she kept her word.

At his mother's urging, Artem reluctantly took the entrance exam to attend Stuyvesant High, a public school with "deep roots" in mathematics, science, and technology. He had always been more of a free spirit than a scientific nerd. Not surprisingly, to himself, at least, Artem flunked the entrance exam. The fallback was to matriculate at Canarsie High School, near the family home, which Artem did in September. Canarsie High was known for its high dropout rate and fractious student body.

On a fateful night in June 1948, Artem tagged along with one of his friends, Sal DeLuca, to a graduation party at the apartment of a classmate, Stella Rossini, in nearby Canarsie. With the help of his older brother, Benny, Artem acquired and brought the obligatory bottle of whiskey. This unchaperoned gathering was supposed to be the party of all high school parties. Girls came smeared with lipstick and sporting highly coiffed hair, eager to have both messed up quickly by an alpha male. Unlimited servings of well-spiked punch would spur this along by easing inhibitions and wiping away unwelcome flashbacks of overstepped moral bounds.

"Hi, Sal," Stella said as she opened the door to Apartment 604. "Who is this cutie you brought with you?"

"This is my friend Artem," replied Sal. "He's the neighborhood fixer-in-training, in all senses of the word. You want to persuade a bully in the neighborhood to leave you alone, he knows how to find the right guy to underscore the point. He can get you a fine watch on the cheap. You need someone to vouch for your whereabouts when you don't want your nonna to know where you've been, he's your guy—a real mensch in his neck of the woods, and polite to the elders. Artem also happens to be a good carpenter. Like his older brothers, he can build a new kitchen table or a backyard fence."

"Nice to meet you, Artem," said Stella. "Come on in, boys, and help yourself to some scrumptious punch."

"Don't mind if we do," said Sal as he and Artem sauntered into the dining room, where an elaborately cut crystal punch bowl was filled not with Christmas eggnog but with an innocent-looking concoction of orange juice, other juice blends, whiskey, and any number of unknown stronger substances.

While seemingly harmless, that was the start of a night to remember. Two girls near the punch bowl handed Artem and Sal their drinks and asked if they wanted to skedaddle to someplace more comfortable. Of course, the boys said yes. Maria, the buxom brunette, winked at Sal, who followed her into a bedroom. Lucille, the skinnier of the two and with auburn hair, took Artem's hand as she and Artem walked behind. Artem had brought a few roofies, which he promptly dropped into the girls' drinks. "I've got dibs on Maria," Sal whispered to Artem.

"If you must," Artem mouthed back.

Soon things were in full swing in the bedroom, with lots of noise coming from all the participants. It was drowned out, however, by the increasing pitch in the living room, where there were now at least twenty other students, who were drinking up a storm while Peggy Lee's "Mañana (Is Soon Enough for Me)" blared on the Victrola. Suddenly there was a pounding on the front door. Stella opened it a crack and saw Officer O'Toole from the apartment down the hall.

"What's going on in there?" Officer O'Toole asked.

"Just some friends getting together," said Stella.

"Where are your parents?"

"Away until tomorrow."

"In that case, I'm coming in," Officer O'Toole said.

He entered, turned off the Victrola in the living room, and said, to no one in particular, "I see you kids are having a blast."

"You wouldn't know, Daddy-O," murmured one nerdy-looking boy, probably too quickly.

Officer O'Toole then pointed at the boy and said, "YOU—do you want a knuckle sandwich?"

"No sir," the boy answered.

"Then keep your fat trap shut," Officer O'Toole admonished. He instructed all the kids in the living room to sign their names in his black book. As they were doing so, Officer O'Toole heard the noise in the bedroom. His ears perked up, and he burst in, catching Sal, Artem, and the girls naked and the girls almost comatose. "Well, look who's here—the son of my friend Leonard from the Rotary," Officer O'Toole said to Artem. "I'll let you off easy this one time by only telling your father," he added.

That was the end of Artem's youth. Artem's mother was far angrier than his father when he told her. "I failed as a mother," she said. "I never should have let you go to Canarsie High, where the big men on campus are the boys who like to get drunk and are going nowhere in life. If only you could have gone to Townsend Harris, like Jonas Salk and that songwriter—what's his name? Oh yes, Ira Gershwin—you might have been able to make something of yourself."

After graduation, Artem continued to live at home. He paid rent and tried to bend to his mother's wishes a bit. He would shower immediately after work, removing all the sawdust collected through odd jobs as a carpenter, usually arranged by one of his older brothers. If Artem was home for dinner, he would take the dishes to the sink and sometimes even wash them. If he went out with friends or on a date, he would promise to be home by 11:30 p.m., except on weekends. He started to remember special occasions and would bring his mother flowers, sometimes for no reason. And perhaps of most impact, he would try to be home for Shabbat dinner, when his mother would light the candles in the sterling silver candlesticks brought over to America from Kiev by her own mother.

In the late 1940s, New York City began its inexorable rebirth from the Depression and World War II. Construction of the United Nations headquarters began. Modern skyscrapers were planned. Robert Moses began his quest to link boroughs by tunnels and highways. And the big band jazz scene welcomed everyone. Artem loved to go into Manhattan with friends to hear Cab Calloway at Café Zanzibar and Charlie Parker and Dizzy Gillespie at the Royal Roost. Taking advantage of these offerings, of course, took money. Artem supplemented his income with occasional off-the-book sales of booze and cigarettes.

At private parties, Artem and his friends would drink heavily, listen to jazz on the Victrola, and, of course, score with women if they could. Artem never had a steady girlfriend.

Things changed abruptly in June 1950, when Artem was called up to serve in the army in the first wave of Korean War draftees. His mother was scared but looked at this as a blessing—perhaps serving the country would force him to assume some responsibility. Artem viewed the military as an opportunity to see new places and have fun with his buddies.

CHAPTER THREE

When launched in 1952, SS *Andrea Doria* was referred to as the most magnificent passenger ship in the world. The Italian government had commissioned her and her sister ship, the SS *Cristoforo Colombo*, after World War II to restore Italy's reputation as a leader in world commerce, especially in the maritime area. The ship was named after Admiral Andrea Doria, a Genoese prince and statesman who in 1528 had led an amphibious assault that drove the French out of Genoa and reestablished the Republic of Genoa after more than a century's domination by foreign powers.

Andrea Doria was 697 feet in length and 29,100 gross tons, designed to cross the Atlantic at twenty-three knots. She was slightly shorter and much lighter than other passenger ships plying the Atlantic, such as SS *Queen Mary*, SS *Queen Elizabeth*, SS *United States*, and SS *Ile de France*. The ship's lightness and shorter length meant she was highly maneuverable, relatively speaking. Although no one dared call her "unsinkable" like SS *Titanic*, they did consider her to be extremely safe. She was divided into eleven watertight compartments by steel bulkheads. In accordance with requirements of the 1948

Convention for the Safety of Life at Sea (SOLAS), she was designed to remain afloat even with two adjacent compartments flooded. This construction theoretically ensured that a ship would list no more than seven degrees, but *Andrea Doria* was designed to survive a list of fifteen degrees. (Experts termed a list of twenty degrees or more "an almost unimaginable calamity" that no ship could survive.) *Andrea Doria*'s double bottom provided added safety, inhibiting damage from obstacles that might pierce the hull from below.

Of perhaps most importance, *Andrea Doria* had two state-of-the-art radar screens to scan the seas for nearby foreign objects, a radio direction finder to help with triangular navigation, and LORAN (long range navigation) equipment operated at low frequencies to afford readings at a range of 1,500 miles, with an accuracy of 10 miles. Of course, great efforts were also put into fireproofing the ship. Flame-retardant insulation was used in nearly all interior spaces, automatic doors could quickly seal off sections in the event of a fire, and the ship had a small fire brigade.

Should calamity ever strike, passengers could be evacuated quickly by sixteen aluminum lifeboats, two emergency boats each capable of holding 58 passengers, two motorized boats each with a 70-passenger capacity, and twelve Flemish lever boats each capable of carrying 168 people. The evacuation capacity provided by those boats was 2,008 souls, above the 1,241 passengers and 560 crew members the ship was designed to carry.

Early in the morning of July 17, 1956, Captain Piero Calamai, a seasoned seaman and sturdy six-footer, began to welcome passengers on board *Andrea Doria* in Genoa for the ship's planned voyage to New York via Cannes, Napoli, and Gibraltar. Ensconced in the first-class foyer on the foyer deck, he focused on the first-class passengers who would occupy the cabins on the boat, upper, and foyer decks and mingle in the lavish surroundings of the fifteen first-class public rooms, including the Belvedere Observation Lounge on the boat deck, directly below the bridge, adorned with a larger-than-life bronze statue of Admiral Doria. The ship was as opulent as anything at sea and Italian through and through, with a colorful modern edge. On prior voyages Captain Calamai had welcomed the likes of Tennessee Williams, Cary Grant, Orson Welles, Spencer Tracy, Kim Novak, Joan Crawford, Elizabeth Taylor, John Steinbeck, and Clark Gable.

After sailing from Genoa, *Andrea Doria* arrived in Cannes around midafternoon the same day. No dock was large enough to accommodate her, so she was moored about 150 yards offshore. Mahogany-clad Riva tenders brought passengers to the ship from Le Vieux Port. To those forty-eight individuals waiting on the dock, the ship looked sleek and majestic, with the sun gleaming down on its black hull and brilliant white deck and trim. Captain Calamai waited patiently aboard the ship to greet those traveling in first class, the women adorned in Chanel, Hermès, and Givenchy while the men looked alike in blue blazers and white slacks.

"Welcome, Miss Roman," Captain Calamai said. "It's so good to see you again. Welcome aboard! And it's little Dickie, isn't it? He's such a sweetheart. I loved your performance in *Strangers on a Train*. Oh, and I thought you and Ronnie Reagan were going to make a fine couple, but I guess he wasn't marriage material, eh?" Ruth Roman had been dating Mr. Reagan after her first divorce but ended up marrying a man from a well-heeled newspaper family, whom she divorced just four months prior to the July 1956 voyage. Born in Lynn, Massachusetts, to Lithuanian-Jewish immigrant parents, she had made a giant leap to become a Hollywood starlet.

"Oh, Captain, how lovely to see you too," she said while offering a limp hand. "I see you haven't lost your Italian sense of humor since we last sailed together. I'm a mere thirty-three years old and already have had considerable life experiences, so I'm not fazed by your wit."

At dusk, after the guests had finished boarding and settled into their cabins, *Andrea Doria* left port, bound for Napoli, and the journey of all journeys was underway. Ruth Roman had taken two adjacent cabins on the starboard side of the upper deck, numbers 82 and 84, one for herself and the other for Dickie and his nurse. She immediately befriended her cabin 80 neighbors, Richardson Dilworth, mayor of Philadelphia, and his wife, Ann, who was in a foul mood because she had been planning to attend a royal luncheon in Monte Carlo with Princess Grace, the former Grace Kelly of the Philadelphia Kellys. Prince Rainier had required the presence of the princess in Paris, resulting in cancellation of the luncheon.

As *Andrea Doria* was leaving the lights of Cannes in the distance, Miss Roman invited the Dilworths to join her for cocktails in the Belvedere Observation Lounge. They readily accepted, and the three of them sauntered down the grand staircase to the boat deck, where the ship's main lounge was located. Ruth was wearing a smart salmon chiffon dress draped over one shoulder. It was complemented by an exquisite pair of dangle earrings, each centered by an enormous oblong sapphire (contrasting dramatically with her bright red lipstick) surrounded by a row of diamonds and adorned with three hanging pendants, each holding a one-inch circular cluster of diamonds and sapphires. My god, the earrings must have been worth a king's ransom. As the Dilworths and Miss Roman entered the lounge, the maître d' escorted them to a table on the port side with stunning views of the French and Italian Riviera coastlines. Almost magically, a steward with a nametag reading "Art" appeared, taking Miss Roman's order and returning shortly thereafter with a waiter carrying a bottle of Veuve Clicquot champagne and a plate of crudités, which the guests thoroughly enjoyed.

Later that evening, after the guests had dined and the waitstaff had finished their shifts, Art went to the stern for a smoke. He ran into his boss and the first-class head waiter, Valentino Rosin, known onboard the ship as Val, and they struck up a conversation. Art didn't know much about Val's background, so he asked him about it. Val told Art that he'd grown up Jewish in Trieste, Italy. In 1926, at the age of seventeen, he got a job as steward on a passenger ship plying the Mediterranean and North Atlantic. After working on several other ships, he ended up with a job on the Italian ship *Saturnia*, which operated between Trieste and New York until 1940. Valentino came from a mercantile Jewish family which had managed to escape to Switzerland right before the Nazi crackdown in Italy. Fluent in English as well as Italian, he was a prize catch for the Italian

Line, which wanted to cater to its well-heeled *Andria Doria* passengers and hired him in 1953. By that time his entire family had emigrated to Melbourne, Australia, and now ran a bistro in a fashionable beachside resort called St. Kilda.

"I served Ruth Roman, the actress, this evening," Art said. "She's more beautiful in person than she is on the screen. She smelled quite enticing as I leaned over her breasts to place her lobster in front of her. I'd love to try to befriend her, if you know what I mean."

"You must be *meshuggeneh*," Val said. "If the captain finds out, he'll throw you off the ship at the next port of call, if not sooner. Our kind—the help, I mean, not Jews—is aboard to cater to the whims of the clientele, not the other way around."

"But I'm so personable," answered Art. "I'll tread carefully so there can be no misunderstanding about my honorable intentions."

Late in the afternoon the next day, Art appeared outside upper deck cabin number 82 and knocked on the door. In his right hand was a bountiful fruit basket, which he told Miss Roman was a gift from the head steward when she answered the door. Miss Roman told him to place it on the writing desk, which he did. Art took the opportunity to tell Miss Roman that he was an admirer of hers and thought she performed wonderfully in all her various movies. She thanked him and said the voyage was intended to be a welcome break from her hectic work schedule and challenging personal life. "Can you understand that?" she asked.

"Of course," he responded. "There is something comforting about watching blue waves as far as you can see for hours at a time."

"How did you end up working on this ship?" Miss Roman continued.

"I came to Europe three years ago, after serving in the Korean War, with the intention to travel around, see the sights, and meet some interesting people," he said. "During my two years wandering about Paris, Madrid, Barcelona, Milan, and Rome, I had success on all fronts. With the value of the local currencies so low, it was easy to live well on the money I had brought. My supply, however, eventually ran out. Fortunately, I had met the daughter of one of the owners of the Italian Line at a nightclub in Rome, and she convinced her father to get me a job as a steward on the ship. I learned a lot about wines during my travels and was able to make a good impression at my interview. That was about a year ago."

"Tell me about your family," said Miss Roman.

"My mother and father entered the United States from a small town near Kiev in the early 1920s with my oldest brother, Ihor. They were Jewish, and times were tough in the ghetto. My father got work in the New York garment industry. They lived in Brooklyn in an area made up mostly of Jewish and Italian immigrants. Two more boys were born, and then came me. My father has done well enough to buy his own home. My mother is the typical Jewish mother—a bit overbearing, but she makes the best latkes, which are potato…"

"I know what they are," Miss Roman interrupted. "We have a lot in common. My parents are European Jews who escaped from the Nazis. They were somehow able to make it to Lynn, Massachusetts, where I was born and raised. I eventually was able to take a long trip to Hollywood, where I got a taste for the finer things in life."

"An amazing story and coincidence," said Art.

An awkward silence enveloped the stateroom. Art moved closer and took one of Miss Roman's hands, saying, "You know, I could get to like you..."

"Hold your horses," shrieked Miss Roman as she backed up a step. She then took a moment to compose herself before continuing. "You are a handsome kid and seem sweet, but you're way too young for me, even after a little bubbly. I get that your hormones are raging, and I, myself, can feel a little tingling. But nothing is going to happen between us. Ever."

Art thought about protesting but remembered what Val had said to him the day before: the possibility of leaning in and kissing her, on the one hand, or losing his job, on the other, or, even worse, being fed to the fish in the Mediterranean. He decided to chalk this one up to experience and leave romancing the actress to his fantasies.

So Art set about trying to be the best steward he could be. One of the cabins he was assigned to oversee was occupied by a young couple from Grenoble, France, on their honeymoon. Thierry de Villiers looked to be in his early thirties and was tall and well-built and dressed quite nicely, as would be expected. His wife, Aline, had styled blond hair and was quite attractive, wearing a hint of Chanel No. 5 and a wardrobe curiously leaning more toward Givenchy than Chanel. Art knew that only because he had snooped in her wardrobe one morning when the de Villiers were away from their stateroom, and he was freshening it. The couple spoke only French, and Art's knowledge of that language was rudimentary. While Art had been required to study French in high school, he'd never taken to it as he did to the girls in his class who were competing for his attention. He tried his best to communicate his wish to be of any assistance they might require. "Puis-je être utile aujourd' hui?" he would ask, hoping for a "no merci" response. On one occasion, when madame was away from the cabin, Thierry answered "S'il vous plaît, je desire une bouteille de Perrier et une vache qui rit." Not realizing that M. de Villiers was requesting a particular brand of cheese with his sparkling water, Art responded by asking, jokingly, in his pidgin French, "voulez vous au lieu d'une putain de vache?" Taking offense to the flippant inquiry whether he might prefer a fat whore, M. de Villiers asked Art to leave immediately.

Over the next few days, *Andrea Doria* made its planned stops at Napoli and Gibraltar, picking up more passengers, who spawned more reverie. Bringing the ship in and out of the Port of Gibraltar was a navigational challenge because Gibraltar is located on a spit of land to the east side of the Bay of Gibraltar, a body of water hollowed out of Spain just before the Mediterranean turns into the Strait of Gibraltar. The bay's area is small and highly congested with shipping traffic, so the helmsman had to strictly observe the channel markers, keeping the red nuns to starboard on the way in and to port on the way back out to sea. The radio operator also had to listen closely for messages sent from nearby ships. Vigilance was key.

After leaving Gibraltar and heading through the Strait of Gibraltar, *Andrea Doria* headed into the unpredictable North Atlantic, where she encountered several days of storms. Nick and the other stewards were harried, ministering to the ship's many seasick passengers.

When passengers awoke on Tuesday, July 24, 1956, *Andrea Doria* had finally entered calm waters. Passengers began to emerge from their cabins, and normalcy gradually returned. Art was assigned to the ship's dinner service, where he looked sharp in his dinner jacket. As he scanned the room, he took note of all the elegance. Men were smartly attired, many wearing Patek Philippe wristwatches, the latest fashion. The women were all in evening dresses and adorned with precious jewels. Actress Betsy Drake showed off the gleaming diamond necklace given to her by her husband, Cary Grant. It was part of a collection valued at $250,000, equivalent to $2.5 million in today's dollars. Ruth Roman wore a pair of the conspicuous and expensive earrings for which she was known. Clipped to each ear was a dark blue sapphire that must have been the size of a walnut. It was surrounded by small diamonds. Each earring had three plummeting strands of diamonds, and there was a cluster of diamonds and sapphires at the bottom of each of those. The pair must have been worth at least $100,000. It was hard to avoid staring at them. A mere fleeting glance at the earrings created a sense of envy and a lump in one's throat.

On the afternoon of July 25, 1956, the seas remained calm, but patches of fog began to roll in, eventually forming a ubiquitous white latticework quilt. In a firsthand account, Pierette Domenica Simpson said, "Our spirits were covered with a gloomy blanket of fog that even permeated the corridors. For fear of getting lost, passengers spent the day mostly in their cabins packing their suitcases."[1] She continued, "After we attended our last supper on board, my grandparents took me for a short walk on deck. But the fog's condensation made strolling a slippery affair, and the phantom puffs between us made visibility impossible."[2] It is hard to imagine the variety of emotions felt by the passengers in that environment, but fear probably was not one of them. Most undoubtedly looked forward to disembarking in New York early the following morning. Some, like the Dilworths, had their storied lives in Philadelphia ahead of them. For Barbara Boggs, daughter of Chicago department store magnate Marshall Field III, the future was less certain. She had all the money in the world, but her marriage was less than ideal, and she suffered from depression.

Two young Hungarian ballet stars, Istvan Rabovsky and wife Nora Kovach, were looking forward to returning to freedom in the United States, where they had lived only a short time. In May 1953, they had traveled to East Berlin from Budapest with the Hungarian Ballet to perform. When in East Berlin, they learned there was a subway stop beneath their hotel. While other performers were donning their costumes, they slipped into the station and took a subway to West Berlin, where they defected.

Betsy Drake focused primarily on her messy personal life. She had boarded the ship in Gibraltar after a tumultuous trip to Spain to confront Cary Grant about his affair with his co-star, twenty-one-year-old Sophia Loren, and the discussion had not gone well. Drake left Spain for Gibraltar the next day to board *Andrea Doria* for her trip home. Years later, she told others she had had a premonition that something bad was about to happen, but she believed that Grant would be the object of the omen.

As on *Titanic* and subsequent transatlantic liners, activities in *Andrea Doria*'s wheelhouse were not observable by the ship's passengers. On the afternoon of July 25, as the ship was approaching the waters off Nantucket, the officers noted that the fog was thickening, which was unsurprising, as the ship was in a spot where the cold Labrador current collided with the warmer Gulf Stream. The ship passed nearby the Nantucket Lightship, a floating lighthouse built in 1936 to provide ships with a navigational signal, a beacon of light visible for twenty-three miles in clear weather, and a foghorn that could be heard for fourteen miles. On this day, the Nantucket Lightship was reporting fog. There was a standard protocol in situations such as this, and Captain Calamai followed it, ordering the posting of a watch officer on one of the two radar screens and an additional lookout on the bow. The twelve watertight compartments below A deck were closed, sealing the space below deck into eleven watertight compartments. The ship's fog whistle was turned on, leading to a somber sound each one hundred seconds. SOLAS also required that every vessel in fog "go at a moderate speed, having careful regard for the existing conditions and circumstances." Captain Calamai ordered an almost risible speed reduction from 23 to 21.8 knots, which probably was in violation of the regulation, but it was in keeping with the standard practice of transatlantic ocean liners, whose owners repeatedly reminded their captains of the ever-present need to keep to the ship's schedule. A slight delay in the ship's arrival would skew the carefully choreographed dance of directing passengers off the ship, cleaning cabins, refueling, replenishing the ship's stores and, ultimately, departing with newly boarded passengers.

Around the time Captain Calamai took these measures, another liner, *Stockholm*, was passing Fire Island on its way to Oslo. Built in 1948, *Stockholm* was only 524 feet long and carried a maximum of only 534 passengers and 208 crew members. Because she plied the Baltic, her bow had been reinforced to cut through ice. She was heading on her normal course toward Nantucket, but this set the ship twenty miles north of the eastbound lane recommended by the 1953 North Atlantic Track Agreement among certain shipping companies. Neither the Italian Line nor the Swedish American Line was a signatory, and even for signatories, compliance was voluntary, not compulsory. However, Swedish Royal Decree No. 581 of 18 July 1952 had required all Swedish vessels to follow North Atlantic Track Agreement routes, so *Stockholm* apparently was violating Swedish law.

On July 25, 1956, at 11:11 p.m., passengers aboard *Andrea Doria* heard or awoke to the cacophony of a massive collision on their ship, which then was forty-five miles south of Nantucket. *Stockholm* had slashed into the starboard bow of *Andrea Doria* at an almost ninety-degree angle, ripping open a forty- or fifty-foot-wide hole across seven of the eleven decks, including cabin numbers 42 through 58 of the upper deck. The collision also ruptured *Andrea Doria*'s fuel tanks and two of her watertight compartments, spewing hundreds of tons of a mix of fuel and water into the lower deck corridors. According to Pierette Domenica Simpson, gathered with her relatives and other shipmates in the upper deck lounge, "We swayed rigidly from an abrupt jolt accompanied by a thunderous noise. Those who were on the outer deck witnessed startling fireworks created by grinding steel—sparked by an unidentified vessel slamming into our hull at full speed. They watched in horror as the perpetrator tried to withdraw from the hole it had created, slicing through thick walls of steel that had once protected passengers from the dangers of the ocean."[3]

Art had finished his evening shift and was smoking a cigar with a few of the other crew members near the stern on the sun deck when the collision occurred. Caught off guard, he was thrown about six feet into one of the lifeboats, where he hit his head and fell to the ground. He noticed blood coming from his right arm and felt a big lump on the right side of his head.

"What the hell!" Art screamed.

"Something awful must have happened," another crew member, Terry from Derry, said.

"You think?"

"Maybe one of the engines exploded," said Terry. "That would explain the noise and the sudden movement."

Just then, there was a break in the fog. The group could see the outline of what looked like a large white creature ahead in the distance to starboard. "Holy crap," Terry said. "It's a ship. Must have hit us. What are we going to do?"

"Our jobs, idiot," said Marco, another member of the crew. "We need to listen for orders from the captain and follow them. We may need to man the lifeboats. This is what we trained for."

Andrea Doria continued to move forward for 2.6 nautical miles with *Stockholm* lodged in its hull. Because the captain of *Stockholm* had issued "stop engine" and "full astern" orders immediately before the collision, *Stockholm* withdrew from *Andrea Doria* slightly, but not without ripping open her hull "with the force of a giant can opener, as it smashed portholes and side ports, widening the breach ruinously."[4]

Then all hell broke loose. Passengers in public areas ran to their cabins to locate loved ones. There, they donned life jackets and proceeded to their assigned muster or way stations on the promenade deck. There, they expected to receive further instructions, which never came. Unlike other lines, the Italian Line did not preassign passengers to individual lifeboats. There had been only one lifeboat drill, after the Napoli stop, meaning that passengers boarding the ship in Gibraltar had no instructions about what to do in an emergency.

Inside the ship, the corridors were full of panicked passengers running this way and that, pushing past one another while trying to figure out where to go. They were impeded by smoke from fuel that had caught fire and slippery, oil-blackened water flowing on the lower decks. Passengers also had to deal with the listing of the ship, which was recorded at eighteen degrees immediately after the collision and soon reached twenty-two degrees. *Andrea Doria* was not engineered to withstand such a list; seawater from two breached compartments would begin to flood the remaining watertight compartments and eventually capsize and probably sink the ship.

At that point, there was only one realistic remaining hope. The collision had breached all five fuel tanks in the double bottom on the starboard side. The five tanks on the port side, however, remained intact and were empty because their fuel had been used during the voyage. Filled only with air, they acted as a balloon, pushing up the port side of the ship and pushing the starboard side further into the sea. Opening the port tanks would allow water to enter, partially offsetting the ship's list to starboard. The chief engineer, however, concluded there was no way to flood the port fuel tanks with seawater.

On the port side of the lido deck immediately below the bridge, crew members tried in vain to release the eight lifeboats from their davits. Because the ship had been designed to withstand a list of up to fifteen degrees, the lifeboats had been designed to be launched at up to a fifteen-degree list. At the greater list reached quickly after the collision, launching those lifeboats proved impossible. Many passengers, however, continued to hover on the port side, thinking the high side was safer. There is no indication that they ever received instructions to go to the starboard side, where lifeboats were being launched.

As passengers with orange life vests were trying to get into lifeboats, so, too, were the ship's service crew members. Easily seen in their contrasting gray life vests, they were pushing through the corridors and ultimately securing seats on the first lifeboats departing *Andrea Doria* for one of the six nearby ships that had answered the SOS. Art, the steward, was one of them, but before reaching the promenade deck he decided to check the upper deck, one deck below, for which he had been assigned responsibility in the event of an emergency. His job in an emergency such as this was to ensure no one was left behind in any of the upper deck cabins.

"Should I start on the port or starboard side?" he mused. The port side was probably the safest, as it was away from the side of the collision and highest above the water. On the other hand, water pouring in from the hole on the starboard side of the ship was unlikely to reach all the way up to the upper deck, and passengers still in their cabins on the starboard side were likely to need more assistance than those on the port side. So he decided on starboard.

He entered the stairwell from the grand ballroom on the promenade deck and took the grand staircase down one level to the upper deck, where he emerged on the starboard side in front of cabin number 42. He rapped on the door three times with his fist. There was no answer, and the door was locked. He used his master key to open it. The cabin was empty, so he moved aft to the next cabin, number 44, which also was unoccupied.

Not so with cabin number 46. After Art knocked, Colonel Walter Carlin opened the door with a dazed expression as he pointed to the sleeping quarters behind him. The exterior wall had been ripped away and was exposed only to the cold night air. Colonel Carlin's wife, Jeanette, had been in bed near the exterior wall and was swept away during the collision. Art clasped Colonel Carlin gently by the hand, retrieved his life preserver, and placed it over his head and directed him to the stairwell leading to the promenade deck. Colonel Carlin said he was OK and could make it to his muster station.

Art found upper class cabin numbers 48 and 50 to be empty. He couldn't unlock the door of cabin number 52, which was occupied by two young half sisters, Linda Morgan and Joan Candara. Linda had landed on the deck of *Stockholm*, seriously injured. Joan had been swept away in her bed into the abyss.

Working his way aft, Art knocked on each cabin door as he reached it. If no one answered, he used his master key to gain entry. Several cabins held individuals who had been pinned down and injured by the collision. For these, Art joined in group efforts started by others to free the victims.

Upon reaching cabin numbers 82–84, Art saw a door ajar, and no one inside. That's Ruth Roman's cabin, he quickly recalled. Art then spotted something glittering under the lamp on the night table. It was the same pair of earrings she had worn on the night he first served her. In her haste to escape, she must have left them behind.

The sight jolted Art's moral compass. He could grab the earrings and continue down the starboard corridor looking for survivors, with the expectation of returning them to Miss Roman on shore. Or he could pocket them for himself, secure in the thought that Miss Roman would assume they went down with the ship. It was a difficult dilemma until it wasn't. "Wait a minute," he mumbled. "I can just take them now and decide later what to do with them. How could I have been so stupid as to slow myself down with a moral dilemma in a time like this? That's the way to go."

With the earrings stuffed in his pants pocket, Art continued down the corridor, finding only a few more guests in their cabins. He instructed them to go to the promenade deck and told them how to get there. Suddenly, about ninety minutes after the collision, *Andrea Doria* leaned sharply to starboard again. The list was now about twenty-seven degrees, just too much for most to take. Art decided it was time to save his own skin. He took the aft stairwell up one level to the promenade deck, where passengers on the port side were obeying Captain Calamai's recent order to forsake the port lifeboats in favor of those on the starboard side. Art emerged on the promenade deck to this utter chaos created by the passengers and many crew members trying to make their way into too few lifeboats. "Better jump in one," he said to himself, and he did.

The ships called to lend assistance were just arriving, and the first three lifeboats were being lowered. In view of the list, this was a difficult process, and the boats were far from *Andrea Doria*'s starboard side. People were trying to lower themselves on ropes. Art was able to lower himself into the boat just before it pushed away from *Andrea Doria*. It was one of the first three boats to reach *Stockholm*, which was accepting *Andrea Doria* lifeboats after its own engineers had found it seaworthy even with the hole in the bow. When he saw that the boats were half empty and most occupants were men wearing the gray uniforms of the *Andrea Doria* service crew, the captain of *Stockholm* was incredulous.

A total of five ships powered to the collision area to assist after receiving an SOS from *Andrea Doria* at 11:20 p.m. These ships, along with the badly damaged *Stockholm*, were able to rescue 1,660 *Andrea Doria* passengers and crew members. The SS *Ile de France* alone rescued 753 of them, including Betsy Drake and Ruth Roman. *Andrea Doria*'s death toll was forty-six passengers (plus five *Stockholm* crew members perished). Many of the survivors watched in amazement as *Andrea Doria* sank at 10:09 a.m.

In a law school class on maritime law many years later, I learned considerably more about what went wrong in the lead-up to the collision. The official inquest reached no conclusions, and liability was never established in court because both *Stockholm* and *Andrea Doria* were insured by Lloyds of London, a fact that drove an out-of-court settlement. However, it seems clear that applicable regulations were too vague and that both ships made mistakes.

One mistake involved use of the lanes recommended in the North Atlantic track. *Andrea Doria* was in the correct lane, even though it was not required to use that lane, and *Stockholm* was traveling too far north in order to shave off time to Gutenberg, as was its normal practice. Another, made by both ships, was traveling at too great a speed when fog was impeding visibility. Yet another mistake made by both was inadequate use of the latest navigational equipment, which should have given earlier and better information about sightings of the other vessel as course corrections were made, some at the last minute. Communication channels between ships were inadequate; indeed, it was not until after the collision that each ship learned the identity of the other. A final major contributor was lack of clarity in the regulation calling for a port-to-port crossing unless the ships are so far to each other's starboard sides that adjusting course for a port-to-port crossing would be dangerous. *Stockholm* was expecting a port-to-port crossing and *Andrea Doria* was expecting a starboard-to-starboard crossing, in part to avoid having to go too close to the dangerous Nantucket shoals.

In the last five minutes before the collision, each ship made multiple course adjustments to apply what it thought was the correct rule for approaching ships and, ultimately, to attempt to avoid a collision. However, ships are heavy and have tremendous forward momentum, even if engines are thrown into reverse. So nothing could be done.

Subsequently, over the years, scuba divers made multiple forays to *Andrea Doria*. The ship's skeleton remains 160 feet below sea level on the bottom of the Atlantic, fifty-three miles southeast of Nantucket, in an area known to mariners as "Times Square" because there was so much sea traffic there.[5]

CHAPTER FOUR

The fall of 1980 was an especially sweet one. In New England, the leaves turned into a vivid array of colors and stayed on the trees almost until Thanksgiving. I had married Rachel Miller several years earlier, thankfully passed the Massachusetts bar exam, and was working as an associate at a Boston law firm that specialized in high-tech business, intellectual property, and maritime law. We lived in an old cottage on Essex Avenue in Gloucester, which we had purchased three years earlier, slightly before the birth of our first daughter. Fresh off a top-tier employee evaluation at the end of August, I was working on some interesting legal assignments, and I was in love. On top of that, the lobsters were in season and abundant.

Rachel had just gotten a job as a six-grade teacher at the Fuller School in Gloucester. She loved kids and dove into her job with the verve of a neophyte educator, spending hours planning perfect bulletin boards and writing attention-grabbing mimeographs for the students. Rachel had a class of twenty—consisting of twelve girls and eight boys—which was typical of public schools at the time. The girls were mostly hipsters, donning laced tops and striped bellbottoms. The boys were, well, boys. They liked the Red Sox, the Patriots, and the Celtics, playing team sports themselves and going fishing. They couldn't have cared less about the girls.

Late on a crystal-clear Monday morning in September, I was doing research in the law firm library, a magnificent space on the thirtieth floor of the Prudential Tower, overlooking Boston Harbor, when I was called to the phone. Rachel was on, and she was upset. Earlier that morning, she had sent her attendance sheet to the school office, noting four student absences that day. Nothing unusual there, but she had then been visited in her classroom by her principal, Mrs. Frye, and two officers from the Gloucester Police Department, who told her that one of those students had been reported missing by her parents. It was Maia Murphy, age eleven.

Maia was a truly gifted student and a natural athlete. She also knew how to be everyone's good friend and never lacked for tablemates at lunch in the cafeteria. The police wanted to question Rachel first and then the students.

Rachel told me she gave everyone a silent reading assignment before she left the room with Mrs. Frye and the police officers, a Detective John Sullivan and Officer Margie O'Rourke. Rachel was escorted into the principal's office and answered the questions posed to her but didn't know anything of relevance. Officer O'Rourke asked her if anything had seemed unusual on Friday, when Maia was last at school, and she said no. Officer O'Rourke wanted to know who Maia's closest friends were, and she answered Carolyn McManus and Wendy Price, both classmates. Did Maia seem happy at home, Detective Sullivan asked? Yes, Rachel said, although Carolyn and Wendy might have more insight. As an afterthought, she reported that Maia had seemed excited about accompanying her family on a charter fishing trip over the weekend from Gloucester Harbor.

Next came the dreaded undertaking of telling the kids in Rachel's class about Maia. Rachel walked back to her classroom, silently and nervously, with Detective Sullivan and Officer O'Rourke. As she entered the classroom, her normal poise returned. "Boys and girls, we have guests, Detective Sullivan and Officer O'Rourke, from the police department," she said. "First, we have something to tell you. As you know, Maia didn't come to school today. Unfortunately, Maia's parents had to call the police last night to say they couldn't find her. The police are looking for Maia and thought some of you might have some information that could be useful."

"Please don't be afraid," Rachel continued. "These policemen are your friends and just want to ask if you know anything. If you don't, that's fine. I'm sure Maia will be found safe and sound, and that this will turn out to be a big misunderstanding. So don't worry."

Rachel herself was plenty worried, however. Six years earlier, Michael O'Gorman, a twelve-year-old boy at the same school, had gone missing and was never seen alive again. His body had been found in 1979 in Manchester-by-the-Sea. Even though that probably had been an unrelated event, Rachel knew a few things from the TV crime shows I watched, and she hated that the chances of finding a missing child (or anyone missing, for that matter) decreased significantly after forty-eight hours. Time was of the essence.

Not without cause, Rachel was also fearful about her own safety. Before we got married and moved to Gloucester, she'd worked in an elementary school in South Dorchester, a low-income neighborhood with a high crime rate. While she was never harmed or attacked, she had been in uncomfortable situations. There was the father who, after hearing in a parent-teacher conference that his son often acted out in class, pointed to the conspicuous gold necklace Rachel was wearing and said he wanted to rip it off her neck. Or the incident when, as acting principal, Rachel had to call 911 to report that a noncustodial father had entered the school with a gun looking for his son. Rachel had to hide under her desk until the Boston police arrived and arrested the individual.

Following Rachel's feigned upbeat introduction, Detective Sullivan and Officer O'Rourke proceeded to question Maia's classmates one by one. Had Maia been seen over the weekend? What were her favorite activities? Were there any places she liked to go to be alone? Had anyone been threatening or exhibited anger toward her? Had there been any suspicious individuals around the school or in the neighborhood? The session was essentially a bust, revealing nothing useful. No suspicious characters were identified. Only Carolyn and Wendy had seen Maia since school on Friday, at a sleepover Friday night at Maia's house. Both girls had been picked up by their parents at Maia's on Saturday morning. Wendy had thought that Maia was going to call her Sunday afternoon to go over some homework, but she never received the call. She didn't think much of it because they were both good students and didn't need to collaborate on homework assignments.

Officer O'Rourke then asked casually how Maia's relationship was with her parents and brothers. That's when things started to get interesting. The girls looked at each other, and Carolyn's expression was quizzical. "Come on," said Officer O'Rourke. "Let's have it. Anything you can tell us will only help our efforts to find Maia. And we don't have to tell Maia's parents what you have to say."

"OK," sighed Wendy. "Maia had a wonderful relationship with her brothers. They looked out for her and protected her when their father ranted, on occasion."

"That's right," added Carolyn. "Mr. Murphy is nice enough to us, but he does have a temper, especially after drinking too much, which he does rather often. A couple of weeks ago, Maia told us the family had been sitting around after dinner, and Mr. Murphy had had a few cans of beer. Maia told him she wanted to go with Wendy's family to the Cape for the weekend. He said no way because Wendy's fifteen-year-old brother, Lance, would be there. He started yelling at Maia, saying he doesn't want her anywhere around Lance because he's an older boy and she dresses too provocatively. He got up from his chair and lunged at Maia, but Tom and Tim both jumped up and stopped their father before he could reach her. Maia left the room in tears."

"Where was Mrs. Murphy when this was going on?" asked Officer O'Rourke.

"She was sitting on the couch and barely moved," said Carolyn. "Maia thinks her mother is terrified of her husband and therefore doesn't try to protect the children. According to Maia, this is a repeat of Mrs. Murphy's own relationship with her parents. Before his death, her father was an alcoholic and abusive. Her mother felt powerless to do anything to improve the situation."

When Rachel told me on the phone what had happened that morning, I needed to calm her down. She was emotionally upended by what could have happened and for the kids in her class. I reminded her it could be nothing—Maia might be found soon—and that we would talk about it later that evening. She said sure.

Our house was small, without a garage. I came in through the front door around 7:30 that evening to find Rachel with a glass of merlot in her hand. She tried to act calm, but I could see how tense she was. "What if they don't find Maia?" she asked. "What if something happened to her?"

I was tempted to say "Oh, she'll be fine," but I knew I couldn't truthfully say that. Instead, I gave her a hug and said, "This isn't your fault, and you have no control over what happens, so just try to be as upbeat as you can for your students."

CHAPTER FIVE

When Maia's father, Kieran, called the police at 8:00 p.m. on Sunday evening, he stated that Maia had left the house after breakfast around 10:00 a.m. to ride her bike in the neighborhood. She regularly did that, and the family thought nothing of it. Around lunchtime, when Maia had not returned, the family began to worry. Maia's mother, Carol, called her brother, Bob, around 2:00 p.m. to ask him to help them search for Maia. Bob lived in Manchester-by-the-Sea and came right over. The family then began to scour the neighborhood. Kieran and Bob headed in their cars in separate directions, with Kieran heading east and Bob west, each driving around winding streets and calling Maia's name. Maia's older brothers, Ryan and Tim, jumped on their bikes and also started searching. Carol stayed home in case Maia showed up. This gave her the opportunity to call the mothers of Carolyn and Wendy, Maia's closest school friends. Neither had any inkling of where Maia might have strayed.

One of Maia's favorite places to hang out with friends was Stage Fort Park, with its gazebo, seaside promenade, and beckoning beaches. For a girl of eleven, this was a storybook setting.

She and her friends often ventured to the park together with a thermos filled with hot tea. They could sit in the gazebo for hours, drinking tea and staring at the sea, pretending they were the wives of sea captains waiting for their husbands and bread-winners to return from Grand Banks fishing trips with trawlers heaped with fresh cod. The get-togethers were idyllic. None of the girls knew anything about the treacherous nor'easters that were prevalent between September and April or the trawlers that were sometimes swamped by massive rogue waves. They certainly were clueless about the vanishing sailors on them.

At about 5:00 p.m., as bright daylight was morphing into a more mysterious gradient of blue gray, the makeshift family team gathered at Maia's home and immediately set out in one car for Stage Fort Park in search of Maia. They found neither hide nor hair of her, but they spotted her small red backpack under a gazebo bench. Where could she have gone? And where was her bike? Would she have left the bike somewhere and then walked to the park? If she had taken her bike to the park and then left, why would her backpack still be there? Was there a simple, innocent answer or perhaps a more sinister explanation?

Reality struck at 7:00 p.m., when the family had neither found nor heard from Maia and exhausted all obvious leads. This could not possibly be happening to the Murphys, Carol thought. Her husband ran the dry goods store on Main Street, which had been in the family for several generations. The family was a stalwart benefactor of Our Lady of Good Voyage Church on Prospect Street, and Kieran was a member of the Gloucester Rotary Club. Carol, a stay-at-home mom, organized church bake sales and had been active in the Fuller School PTA when Ryan and Tim attended.

They could no longer just hope and pray that Maia would return on her own volition, Kieran thought and said to Carol. With tears streaming down her cheeks, Carol agreed. At 7:30 p.m., Kieran picked up the phone and dialed the Gloucester police.

"This is Sergeant Graves," said the desk sergeant. "How can I help you?"

"My daughter has been missing since this morning," Kieran said. "We've looked all around Gloucester and can't find her. We've also called everyone we know who might have seen her. No one has."

"How old is your daughter?" the detective asked.

"She's eleven," Kieran responded, "a sixth grader at the Fuller School."

"When did you see her last?"

"This morning at breakfast. She was on her way out to ride her bike and never came back for lunch."

"What is your address?"

"16 Centennial Avenue."

"I'll send someone right over."

Ten minutes later, Detective John Sullivan and his newbie assistant, Officer Margie O'Rourke, arrived at the Murphy home. Detective Sullivan immediately began to ask questions that started gently but turned into a grilling.

"So Maia left on her bike this morning? Do you know where she was going?"

"No. She frequently rides her bike in the neighborhood but always returns," said Kieran.

"Does she go alone or with friends?"

"It could be either," Kieran answered.

"Which was it this morning?

"I don't know," said Kieran.

"You don't know what your eleven-year-old daughter's plans were—only that she was going out?"

"That's correct," chimed in Carol. "She's a good student and always reliable. We contacted her closest friends, but no one had seen her. She was supposed to do homework this afternoon with Wendy Price, but Wendy never heard from Maia."

"When did you start to get worried?"

"Around lunchtime," Carol answered. "That's when Kieran called my brother, Bob, and we started looking all over Gloucester."

"Where, exactly, did you look?"

"We basically used Washington Street as a dividing line," Kieran said. "I drove all around the area to the northwest, going in and out of streets and calling out for Maia. My wife's brother, Bob, covered the southeast area of Gloucester. My fifteen-year-old son, Ryan, and my thirteen-year-old son, Tim, went out on their bikes looking for Maia. None of us found her. So as we had prearranged, we met back here at 4:00 p.m. to compare notes. Because Maia likes Stage Fort Park, we decided to go there. In the gazebo, we found her backpack, but not her bike."

Detective Sullivan picked up the backpack and placed it in a clear plastic evidence bag he had brought with him. He sealed the bag and handed it to his assistant.

"Has Maia been upset about anything lately?"

"Not that we know of," said Carol. Kieran added that the family had all gone on a fishing charter on Saturday, and that Maia had seemed happy—and unusually carefree—out on the water.

"So you don't think Maia might have run away from home?"

"Oh my God, no," Carol answered. "She's a real homebody, and we love her so much. She loves us so much too. Just the other day, we were talking about sending her to Camp Waziyatah, a Maine sleepaway camp, next summer, and she almost started to cry. She adores being in Gloucester and talks about eventually going to Endicott College in Beverly. Of course, she has a good few years before she will have to make that decision."

"Did you check the bus station?" Detective Sullivan asked.

"No, we didn't think of doing that," Kieran answered. "It seems highly unlikely she would have gone there."

"How about camping in the woods? Might she think of doing that?"

"I highly doubt that," Kieran answered. "She likes the comfort of her own bed, not a hard, leaf-covered surface. She is petrified of bugs and wild animals. In fact, a few years ago we were riding our bikes in Maine and came across what everyone thought was a stick in the road. When the stick started to move and we realized it was a snake, Maia started to shriek, shouting, "Get me out of here!"

"You may recall that I did too," piped in Carol. "We Murphy girls like our creature comforts, like soft blankets, comfy pillows, and delicious food served elegantly.

'What was Maia wearing this morning?" Detective Sullivan asked.

"Jeans, a white shirt, a navy blue Land's End fleece jacket, and white Nike sneakers," Carol answered.

"And how would you describe her bike?"

"It's a vintage Schwinn, with three gears, built for a girl," Tom said. "It's black, with a reflector on the rear bumper and a bell on the handlebars. It's got a lot of scrapes and dings."

"Do you have a recent picture of Maia we can have?" Officer O'Rourke asked.

"Sure," Carol responded. She went to the refrigerator and took off a four-by-six color photograph of a blond girl with an engaging smile and handed it to the officer. "This was taken in school a few months ago as part of the PTA fundraiser."

"So to sum up what we now know," Detective Sullivan interjected, "your predictable, conscientious daughter who loves Gloucester but is uncomfortable in the outdoors has disappeared. Her bike also has vanished. We have her backpack, which her parents found in Stage Fort Park, and can go over its contents back at the station. We have no idea where else she might have gone. We can start to interview her schoolmates and others tomorrow. There could be an innocent explanation for what has happened."

"Yet we can't rule out foul play," Officer Rourke exclaimed, probably too loudly. "As you may know, the chances of finding a missing person diminish considerably after the first forty-eight hours. Perhaps we shouldn't wait until tomorrow to start the man—I mean girl—hunt. Let's call out the dogs tonight."

"Do you think so?" asked Carol.

After casting a disapproving glance at Officer O'Rourke, Detective Sullivan said it probably would be a good idea to begin the official search that evening. And that is what happened. A team of ten police officers combed Gloucester all that night, accompanied by dogs following the sniff of Maia's red backpack. The neighbors heard the commotion and offered to help in the search, which of course Detective Sullivan said would be welcome. They canvassed every inch of Gloucester, including Stage Fort Park, Ravenswood Park, Halibut Point State Park, and the waterfront. By 4:00 a.m., when they stopped searching for the night, there still was no sign of Maia.

CHAPTER SIX

As arranged, Detective Sullivan and Officer O'Rourke showed up promptly at 8:00 a.m., with four cups of Dunkin' Donuts coffee and a dozen jelly doughnuts. They sat around the kitchen table with Kieran and Carol Murphy to go over strategy. First, Detective Sullivan asked, "Can you think of anyone who would want to harm Maia?" The response was no. They then asked whether the Murphys could think of anyone who might want to get back at Kieran or Carol for anything. The only person they could identify was Lefty Quinn, who had bought six sets of foul-weather gear from Kieran's store a few months ago and brought it back all ripped up after a few weeks, saying it was no good. Bestowed with his nickname as a kid after it became apparent his right arm was too short to be of much use, Lefty asked for his money back. Kieran said he couldn't do that because the items looked as though they had been misused, but he would be happy to give Lefty store credit. Lefty flew into a rage, saying Kieran shouldn't have sold him an inferior Asian-made product. In fact, Lefty was mad at himself for not having demanded Topsider gear made in Maine by Sperry. There was no calming down Lefty. He stormed out of the store in a rage and said he was never coming back.

"That seems like a stretch," Officer O'Rourke said, "but we'll check it out. Have you noticed anyone around looking strange? That could provide another form of lead." The only person they could think of was the homeless person hanging around the entrance to the Pier 7 Marina, location of Gloucester Sea Charter Outfitters, the company the family had hired to take them out fishing in the Atlantic on Saturday. The homeless man had been sitting at the business entrance, leaning up against one of the two posts. Kieran said the man was Caucasian and looked to be about forty years old. He was wearing old work boots, a pair of stained, khaki-colored jeans, and a ratty-looking denim jacket. He also had a beat-up baseball cap on backward, with curly brown hair sticking out in all directions. When Maia had seen the man, she had squeezed Carol's hand tightly.

Detective Sullivan then asked about Maia's school friends and teachers. Carol said Maia's best friends were Carolyn and Wendy, mentioned the day before. She loved her teacher, Mrs. Dreyer, but hadn't had such a great experience with Mr. Butcher the year before. Maia thought that Mr. Butcher seemed like a bully. He had demanded academic precision and total subservience. If you whispered to a friend in class or looked away from the blackboard, God help you. Although he never lost his temper, he put you down in front of everyone. Maia thought if Mr. Butcher had had the authority to hit the children with a switch, he would have used it.

Detective Sullivan told the Murphys that he and Officer O'Rourke planned to go to school that morning to start interviewing children, teachers, and school administrators. Kieran Murphy asked whether the contents of Maia's backpack offered any leads. Detective Sullivan said he was just about to get to that. The backpack contained a clear plastic water bottle, two Hershey's chocolate bars, a pair of blue children's gloves, a red knit scarf, a hairbrush, a scrap of paper, and what appeared to be a diary. Carol said the scarf, hairbrush, and gloves appeared to be Maia's, but she'd had no clue Maia kept a diary. Kieran agreed with his wife. Detective Sullivan said the backpack and items were at a lab being tested for fingerprints. What he did not tell the Murphys was that the police also had found a pack of Marlboro cigarettes and an opened can of Sam Adams, which also were being tested.

Detective Sullivan and Officer O'Rourke then headed to the school to begin their interviews. They started with my wife, Rachel, and quickly moved to Maia's best friends, Carolyn and Wendy. They knew nothing of Maia's whereabouts, they said, but they confirmed that they sometimes went to nearby parks to talk and play. Officer O'Rourke asked about the sleepover the three girls had had on Friday night. They reported eating pizza, watching the movie *The Blue Lagoon* on the VCR, and talking about all sorts of things, including a few cute boys at school. At the top of Maia's mind was the charter fishing trip she and her family had taken that day. She was enthralled. They had left on a thirty-five-foot trawler from Gloucester Harbor, captained by Mark, one of the owner's sons. He was in his early twenties and had fine brown hair. Largely because of the high wind, the waves were about four feet high, Mark told the Murphys. Maia's mother got very seasick and didn't like the trip at all. Maia, however, loved it. She refused to go anywhere near the live worms or fishhooks, but she did hold a pole for a while, not catching anything. That was OK, she said, because she loved just sitting there, letting the wind blow on her face. Her brothers were in heaven (figuratively speaking), putting live bait on the hooks and holding the poles. Shocking everyone aboard the boat, they were able to catch two striped bass and a bluefin tuna before they returned to shore in the late afternoon.

Kieran had been quiet throughout the trip and seemed to be in a funk, Maia told her friends. He let everyone else do the talking. Maia didn't know why.

Carolyn and Wendy relayed all this information to the detective and officer during the interview. Officer O'Rourke asked whether Maia had mentioned a strange-looking man at the Pier 7 Marina. "Oh," Wendy responded, "yes, you must mean Denis. Maia said he was there. Everyone at school knows him. He seems to be harmless, but he often is unshaven and has eyes like a wolf, taking in everything around him. All the girls are scared to get too close to him."

Detective Sullivan and Officer O'Rourke then asked about Mr. Butcher, who had been their teacher in fifth grade. They didn't like him and stayed clear of him outside the classroom. Yet they had no reason to think he was involved in Maia's disappearance in any way.

All the other kids in Mrs. Dreyer's class were interviewed, but none knew anything useful. They also talked to Mrs.

Dreyer, who was distraught but had no information to impart. Their interview with Mr. Butcher was more interesting. He started out belligerently, demanding to know why in the world anyone would think he had anything to do with Maia's disappearance. Detective Sullivan told him to slow down and take it easy. No one was accusing anyone of anything. However, the police were looking for information about where Mr. Butcher had been yesterday. He told them he had taken his son, Jason, on a Cub Scout outing in the woods and was gone all day. He gave Officer O'Rourke the name of the Cub Scout master he was with, and Officer O'Rourke said she would be sure to call him to verify the story.

They then went to Gloucester Sea Charter Outfitters looking for the homeless guy named Denis. He wasn't there, and Mark, the owner's son, said he hadn't been around today. They asked if he knew anything about where Maia Murphy might be.

"Maia, the nice girl I took out on a fishing trip on Saturday with her family?" Mark asked?

"That's right," answered Detective Sullivan.

"I haven't seen her since she left with her family on Saturday afternoon. Has something happened to her?"

"That's what we're investigating. If you see her, or Denis for that matter, please call us right away."

Detective Sullivan handed his card to Mark, who stuffed it in the right front pocket of his jeans.

Detective Sullivan and Officer O'Rourke then drove to the Pier 7 Marina, where they had been told Lefty Quinn worked as assistant dock master. Lefty spied them from his office as they drove up, and his first thought was to avoid trouble by hightailing out the back door. However, reason prevailed, as he said to himself, "What could the Gloucester police possibly want from me?" If they were coming to talk about the expensive navigation system that had been reported stolen from *Sassy Lady*, he had no information to impart. He stayed the course and bellowed "Hello" in his deep voice when the policemen entered his office. They said hello back and that they needed to ask him a few questions. Delving right in, they asked him if he had had words recently with Kieran Murphy. "Oh, you must mean the foul-weather gear incident," Lefty said. "I think I overreacted, but I was so pissed because the jerk sold me a bill of goods. I thought I was buying a quality product, but all six sets I bought for our workers immediately fell apart. It turns out they were made in Japan, so it goes to figure."

"So you weren't angry enough to kidnap Kieran's daughter to exact revenge?"

"No way," Lefty responded.

"Where were you on Sunday?" Officer O'Rourke asked.

"Here at the marina from 9:00 a.m. to 7:00 p.m. Sunday is our busiest day."

"Was anyone working with you?"

"My mates, Jason and Brett. They'll vouch for me if you ask them."

And they did.

Detective Sullivan and Officer O'Rourke visited the bus station again with the picture of Maia they had been given. Each person questioned said he or she had not seen the girl.

After that, the investigation was broadened in typical fashion. Pictures of Maia were run in the *Cape Ann Times* and placed on telephone poles all around town. Sermons at all the local churches mentioned Maia's disappearance and asked anyone with information to contact the helpline number that had been established. The Murphys held press conferences and promised a $25,000 reward to anyone providing credible information about Maia's whereabouts.

Mr. and Mrs. Murphy were both questioned about Mr. Murphy's drinking. He admitted to having an occasional one too many but denied ever lashing out at Maia. He also said he would never in a million years hurt her. He loved her too much, he told the officers. Mrs. Murphy corroborated what her husband said. Detective Sullivan and Officer O'Rourke didn't believe the Murphys for a minute. However, they didn't think that either parent had anything to do with Maia's disappearance, so they decided not to pursue that line of questioning.

Meanwhile, the Gloucester crime lab carefully analyzed the backpack found earlier and its contents. The only fingerprints on any of the items were Maia's. The water bottle contained mostly cranberry juice and a small amount of Smirnoff vodka, probably taken from the bottle Maia's father kept on a shelf in the dining room credenza. The scrap of paper, probably from a newspaper, had a phone number on it: (508) 284-9083. The police attentively examined the diary. Most of the entries were what one might expect of a girl Maia's age: describing her days at school, conversations with friends, and a developing crush on a boy in her class named Bruce. There were a few descriptions of her father's drunken rages and exclamations of how scared she was when they occurred. The last entry, written on the evening before she disappeared, read as follows:

> Today was the best day of my life. My parents, brothers, and I went on a wonderful boat trip from the Pier 7 Marina. Mom had packed a picnic, with turkey and Swiss sandwiches, coleslaw, potato chips, and vanilla cupcakes with strawberry icing for dessert. They were delicious. My brothers were focused on putting bait on the fishing lines (disgusting!) while I was focused on the captain, a handsome man in his twenties named Mark. My father had too many cans of Sam Adams to understand anything. At the end of the trip, I told Mark how much I loved being out on the ocean and that I hoped to be able to do it again. He said he'd take me out any time he was free, and he gave me a piece of paper with a phone number on it.

The police quickly ascertained that the phone number was that of Gloucester Sea Charter Outfitters at the Pier 7 Marina, where Mark worked. Late Monday, they found Maia's bike near the Pier 7 entrance. It had a flat front tire. After dusting the bike for fingerprints, the police found none except for Maia's. Based on the last diary entry and the location of the bike, they brought Mark in for several hours of intensive questioning. Throughout, Mark maintained his initial stance that his intentions toward Maia were honorable. She seemed like a nice girl, taken by things nautical, and that all he meant by giving her the phone number was to convey that he'd be happy to take her out on the boat again sometime for free. The police queried where he had been from 8:00 a.m. until noon on Sunday. He said he was home with his girlfriend, Sarah Roberts, and that the two of them had made the best of their free time, as he didn't need to be to work until 1:00 p.m. The police asked Mark where Sarah worked, and he said the library. Before Mark was released, two other police officers went to the library and questioned Sarah, who confirmed Mark's alibi.

It was time for a press conference, which was held at 1:00 p.m. on Wednesday. The mayor of Gloucester was there with the chief of police, Randall Barnes, and Detective Sullivan.

"Ladies and gentlemen," the mayor began, "I have the sad duty to inform you that one of our community members has gone missing. Her name is Maia Murphy, and she's an eleven-year-old who attends the Fuller School. We have begun an all-out search for her and at this point don't know where she might be. I will turn the microphone over to Detective Sullivan, who will provide details."

"Thank you, mayor. On Sunday evening, Maia's parents contacted our office to report Maia missing. She hadn't been seen since that morning, when she left home on her bike to ride around the community, a common practice of hers. We were unable to locate Maia during an all-night search, in which many neighbors joined. We are in possession her backpack, which her parents had found in Stage Fort Park. Later, we found her bike at the entrance to the Pier 7 Marina.

"We are in the process of conducting an active investigation and would appreciate any information anyone might have about Maia's disappearance or whereabouts," Detective Sullivan continued. "The Murphy family has posted a $25,000 reward for such information. Maia is tall for her age, about five feet, two inches, and has long, wavy blond hair. She was last seen wearing a white cotton top and blue denim jeans. We have a pile of flyers containing Maia's picture down in front for anyone who may be interested. Feel free to reach out to me at police headquarters with any information, or you can call our toll-free hotline, which is (800) 456-9999. Thank you all for your cooperation."

The local newspapers picked up flyers and published stories about Maia and her disappearance, along with her picture. No solid leads were produced.

There was a lot of scuttlebutt going around town about the investigation. Townspeople who did not have jobs typically spent time at a coffee shop on Main Street, drinking their morning cups of joe and eating Pewter Pot muffins. Knowing about the drinking problem that Maia's father, Kieran, had, some thought Kieran must have killed her accidently in a rage and disposed of her body in one of the vast nearby forests. Others thought she might have gone to the bus terminal to take a bus to her grandparents' house on Lake Winnipesaukee to escape her father. One of the newspapers got wind of the existence of Maia's diary and the specific diary entry. Based on that, some thought Mark must be the culprit.

The police did too, notwithstanding Sarah's alibi, and called Mark in for further questioning. They read him his Miranda rights and asked if he would voluntarily answer their questions. He said he would—he had nothing to hide.

However, the questions were tough and relentless.

"How well did you know Maia Murphy?" an investigator asked.

"Not well at all. Sometimes she would come to the marina with her friends, and I would say hi."

"Did you ever try to have sex with her?"

"Wait, no, are you nuts? She is way too young for me. I'm not a pervert."

"Then tell us what happened three years ago, when you worked in town at the minimart. You tried to lure little Sally Owens into the storeroom, didn't you? What were you going to do with—or I should say *to*—her?"

"I have no idea what you're talking about," said Mark.

"Do you know who Sally Owens is?"

"Sure. She was a sweet little girl with a big smile and alluring blond hair. Sometimes she came in, occasionally alone but usually with some friends."

"Sally told the store manager, Mr. Dinsmore, that on one occasion you were talking to her sweetly and asked if she wanted to check out the storeroom. Did you ever do that?"

"No, sir, I did not. I probably was talking to her sweetly because I was *always* nice to her, but you have everything else wrong. As Mr. Dinsmore probably also told you, I was a hard worker with little time on my hands. I never would have had the chance to escort Sally anywhere."

Mark also was probed about what he and Sally usually talked about, but he couldn't remember anything, he said. "Maybe school," he offered tentatively. Then Mark recalled that Sally had a St. Bernard named Rufus, who often ambled along with her on a long leather leash. When Mark explained about Rufus, the investigator's demeanor changed slightly, because Sally had never mentioned bringing her dog. Perhaps Sally wasn't being entirely truthful, the investigator thought. He decided to switch back to the subject of Maia's disappearance, peppering Mark with many of the same questions that had been asked and answered previously.

During the remainder of the inquiry, which lasted well into the evening, Mark stuck to his story. He had not seen Maia at the pier on Sunday. After finishing work, Mark went home and spent the evening with Sarah, a fact that Sarah corroborated.

Three weeks to the day after the first press conference, Detective Sullivan called a second one on the courthouse steps to announce the results of the investigation. He began by expressing the deep sympathy that he and his colleagues had for the Murphy family. The last three weeks had been a real ordeal, he said. The investigation so far had failed to produce a shred of evidence about where Maia might be. Even with searches of nearby parks ongoing every day, nothing had been uncovered. He said various people had been interviewed and nothing suggested that Maia had been subject to foul play at the hands of any individual.

Then the questions began:

"Are you saying you think Maia decided to run off somewhere on her own without telling her parents?" one reporter asked.

"Not at all," Detective Sullivan answered. "It has been exactly three weeks since Maia went missing. Although we haven't found her or her body, the probability is high that she is no longer alive. She could have wandered off somewhere and suffered an accident. Or she might have met a more nefarious ending. We just don't know at this point."

"Will you continue looking for her?" a reporter from WEVS in Nashua, New Hampshire, asked.

"Absolutely," Detective Sullivan responded. "This remains an active investigation and will continue for the foreseeable future. We have sent Maia's fingerprints to the FBI, where they and her name will be placed in a national database of missing persons. The hotline we established for the public to provide information will remain open. If anyone has or obtains any information that might be useful, please let us know."

The vibrant fall leaves fell from the trees, and late 1980 morphed into a dreary 1981. When he was drunk, quoting Shakespeare, Mr. Murphy referred to it often as "the winter of our discontent."

When spring 1981 finally began, Maia still had not been found. Her absence was excruciating for the Murphys and still on the minds of the residents of Gloucester. The official conclusion was that foul play must have been involved, and the police never gave up looking for Maia or the perpetrator. Yet the case was classified as cold. The investigation had focused heavily on Gloucester Sea Charter Outfitters and Mark, especially. Nothing palpable had been discovered during the police interviews. It had been impossible to determine why Maia's backpack was found at Stage Fort Park or why her bike was at the Pier 7 Marina on that ill-fated Sunday.

CHAPTER SEVEN

People around town referred to Mark as enigmatic. Born in October 1958, he was twenty-one years old when Maia went missing. He was the oldest of three brothers and Jewish, which set him apart from most of his friends in Gloucester.

Judaism played a central role in Mark's upbringing. His mother, Sylvia, brought up in Brooklyn in a well-educated Jewish family, had insisted on this. Mark went to Sunday school at the community synagogue in Gloucester and learned Hebrew after school on Tuesdays. When his many Catholic classmates were released early from school every Wednesday to receive catechism instruction, he was envious that they were permitted to skip school while he was not. Nevertheless, as his mother prodded, Mark persevered with his religious studies and became a bar mitzvah early in 1972.

Throughout his school years, Mark was quiet and had only a few close friends. He got along well with everyone, however, and was a solid student. Mark excelled in all things measurable. Not surprisingly, he loved the game of chess and was captain of the chess club in high school. When he was accepted by Northeastern, Mark's parents were jubilant. Although he would go on to live in Cambridge with all the potheads while at school, he never shed his reputation as a geek. During his sophomore year, he met Sarah Roberts at a Boston University mixer. Hailing from Manhattan with an impeccable family pedigree, Sarah was neither beautiful nor animated. However, she had a certain look about her that made Mark light up when he saw her. Petite with short brown hair, she had a smile that could melt a boy's heart. Mark inhaled deeply and asked her if she would like to get together sometime for coffee. Shockingly to him, she said yes. They met the following weekend and hit it off. Providing a counterpoint to his business studies, she was majoring in English with a specialization in medieval literature. On subsequent dates, she would wax poetic about William Langland's *Piers Plowman* and its emphasis on obligation and penitence. Mark didn't care that he barely understood a word Sarah was saying because he loved listening to her melodic voice. He also melted when she told him about *Beowulf*'s recurring struggles of good over evil, thinking about his own recurring dreams of fighting off intruders who entered his bedroom to kidnap him at knifepoint and chain him to a chair in a cabin in the woods. Mark's adoration of Sarah contrasted markedly with the disdain Sarah's prior boyfriends had expressed about anything ethereal coming from her mouth.

Although Mark was adept at learning business principles, his greatest joy was being out on the water on one of his father's fishing boats. The salty sea air cleared your sinuses and had a soothing aroma. The wind typically whipped up late in the afternoon, creating a further sense of separation that calmed the soul. Once Sarah and Mark became a couple, Mark couldn't wait to bring Sarah up to Gloucester and take her out on a boat. She, too, liked being out on the ocean, but not nearly as much as Mark did. She preferred sitting on the front porch with Mark's mother, Sylvia, and telling her about all the wonderful types of knowledge she was garnering in college. Truth be told, Mark's mother only tolerated Sarah. Because she was his first girlfriend, Mark's mother decided it was important to be especially nice. Yet Sylvia didn't understand Sarah's cerebral pronouncements any more than Mark did. Secretly, Sylvia wished her son would dump her and find a nice Jewish girl who would help her make challah and say the Hebrew blessing each Friday evening over the Shabbat candles.

In the summer of 1978, at home in Gloucester after his junior year of college, Mark was able to work as a charter captain on one of his father's boats. He had been offered a job as an intern at a local high-tech company, but he turned it down in favor of his true passion, ocean adventure and discovery. As the eldest son in the family, he had moved to a separate space in the basement of his parents' home, with its own entrance, bathroom, and kitchenette.

It was there that the Gloucester police interviewed Sarah more than two years later, after Maia's disappearance. Because Sarah provided an alibi for Mark, the police never saw the need to obtain a warrant to search the basement premises.

CHAPTER EIGHT

On Saturday night, June 14, 1958, the walls of the ballroom of the St. George Hotel in Brooklyn Heights were strewn with gardenias, white carnations, and baby's breath, while each of the twenty round tables had a massive centerpiece of red roses, pink carnations, and assorted greens. This was probably the most celebrated hotel in Brooklyn, after all, having been designed in grand style decades earlier by noted architect Emery Roth from Austria-Hungary, who also designed many other Manhattan landmarks, including the San Remo, the Beresford, and the El Dorado on Central Park West, the Hotel St. Moritz on Central Park South, and the Oliver Cromwell on West 72nd Street, directly across from the Dakota. The wedding guests were sitting at one end of the room in rows facing the chuppah, also adorned in flowers, awaiting the arrival of the wedding party and, ultimately, the bride herself.

The engraved invitation had said the wedding would start at 7:00 p.m., but all the guests knew that Jewish weddings never start on time. At 7:25 p.m., a string quartet began to play, and the wedding party started the procession. First came the bride's mother on the arm of her eldest son, Richard, then the groom's parents and brothers, followed by grandparents on both sides, the bridesmaids, and their escorts, the groomsmen. Artem had walked to the chuppah from the side in his rented tuxedo and white yarmulke and was standing there next to his best man.

Artem was both nervous and excited. He had met his bride, Sylvia Rothman, a year earlier at a party at the home of a mutual acquaintance in Manhattan. She was a senior at Brooklyn College, majoring in English. Sylvia seemed nice, was reasonably attractive, and had a part-time job as a switchboard operator at Trio, a company selling ladies' undergarments in the Garment District. If she is in college, she must be smart, Artem thought. When he heard that her father was an NYU professor living in Brooklyn Heights, he mused she might be "the one." Artem used all the right moves, telling her of his service to the country in Korea and his narrow escape from death aboard *Andrea Doria*. Sylvia was smitten and ultimately decided that she wanted to marry Artem and bear his children. In January 1958, after taking Sylvia dancing at the Rainbow Room, Artem proposed, and Sylvia accepted. Then came the challenging task of telling Sylvia's parents. Artem was not well educated, and his odd jobs in construction were not impressive. He could not boast (or even tell) of the supplemental income he earned by being a neighborhood fixer. So the two of them devised a plan: they would tell her parents that Artem had decided to better himself by attending the City College of New York full time under the GI bill while Sylvia supported them both temporarily. Eventually, he would graduate and get a good job, and they would be able to start a family. The plan, however, did not go as the couple had intended.

When Sylvia first brought Artem home to dinner to meet her parents, they were cordial but not impressed by his vocabulary or family credentials. At the dinner table, they gave each other knowing looks on each of the two occasions he started a sentence with the word "me" (as in "Me and Sylvia") and once more when he said he "did good" on an exam. Later that night, they remarked to each other that he ought to know better. After Artem and Sylvia announced their engagement, Sylvia's parents voiced their misgivings privately to her, and she responded as one might expect, telling them in a raised voice that they had no right to make decisions for her. It was 1958 and she was a liberated woman!

Artem and Sylvia set the wedding for June 14 and informed her parents, who were not thrilled but decided not to tempt fate by opposing the marriage. Sylvia's father, Arnold, told the couple he would pay for the wedding. He added "Mazel tov" in a less-than-enthusiastic tone. Sylvia's mother, Doris, just smiled wanly. After Artem left, Doris pitched a fit and threatened not to attend the wedding of her beautiful and talented daughter to that loser. Doris herself hailed from a far-flung branch of the Morgenthau family, which had only a modicum of money but lots of pride laced with snootiness.

What could poor Sylvia do in that situation other than tell the truth? She blurted out that she was three months pregnant and needed to get married to safeguard her respectability, and that of her parents. Arnold and Doris were appalled, but the news changed everything,

After taking what seemed like an eternity to get over the shock, Sylvia's parents decided to make lemons into lemonade by throwing an elaborate wedding designed to impress their friends, relatives, and consequential acquaintances. The president of NYU and the chairman of the NYU business department were both there with their wives. So were all the ladies serving with Doris on the board of the New York Chapter of ORT, the Women's American Organization for Rehabilitation through Training (which assisted Eastern European Jews), with their spouses.

When she walked down the aisle on the arm of her father, Sylvia looked positively radiant. The rabbi said a few prayers, led the couple in the marriage vow exchange, and quickly concluded the ceremony. Champagne and canapés were served by strolling waiters wearing white gloves. The famed steakhouse Delmonico's prepared a sumptuous meal of chopped salad, beef Wellington, and baked Alaska. The revelers continued the evening by dancing to the music of the Miles Davis Sextet. Before the band roused the guests' interest in sanding the polished floor with their shoes, a sixteen-year-old duo known as Tom and Jerry played guitar and crooned a few songs for the younger folks in attendance. As part of their repertoire, Tom and Jerry sang "Hey Schoolgirl," which had recently become a nationwide hit. Several years later, the duo would drop their stage moniker and revert to their birth names, Paul Simon and Art (short for "Arthur Ira") Garfunkel.

Following dinner and dancing, the wedding couple retired to the hotel's bridal suite. Artem had collected many envelopes from guests during the evening and couldn't wait to open them, as they contained wedding gifts of cash, typical in the Jewish community. He was hoping for a big haul from the high-rolling friends of the Rothmans but was disappointed when he counted only $3,000. He had not yet gotten anything from either set of Sylvia's grandparents, but they were not rich, so he couldn't count on much. Also, Sylvia's parents had paid for the wedding, so he couldn't expect anything more from them. His own parents probably would give the couple a cash gift, but they didn't have the means to provide a substantial sum. Sylvia, however, didn't care. She had her man, whom she adored. They would live happily ever after with each other in a tenement, if necessary, with their several children.

For the remainder of 1958 and in the winter of 1959, Artem and Sylvia lived in a furnished Brooklyn row house owned by Sylvia's parents. Relying on Artem's sporadic income and Sylvia's small but steady salary from Trio, they were able to pay the rent promptly each month.

In September 1958, four weeks before she was scheduled to deliver her baby, Sylvia was required by her employer to leave her job. That triggered a profound sense of angst in Artem. Would his income suffice to cover the family's expenses? He had a small amount of savings and also knew that his father-in-law wouldn't kick them out of the house if he couldn't pay the rent, but he didn't want to be beholden to him. He had partially mended fences with his in-laws by convincing them he intended to be a good family man and father, and Sylvia's mother was actually excited about the baby, her first grandchild. Yet Artem had no idea how he could follow through. Having to support the family meant he had to shelve the idea of attending City College, and he had no idea how to choose a career.

On one night in February 1959, Sylvia was cuddling Mark while Artem was sitting on the dog-stained couch drinking a beer. He seemed to be in a particular funk. Sylvia asked him what was wrong, and he told her. She was sympathetic and suggested that he call her Uncle Benny, a dentist, for advice. Artem said he would but secretly doubted that Uncle Benny would be helpful. Surprisingly, Benny came through. "I know a guy who owns a button company, and I'll bet he will hire you as a salesman," he said. "He already sponsored and has hired many Jews who were able to escape from Nazi Germany."

Artem started work at the Streamline Button Company in the spring. He had a small base salary that was elevated by commissions. His territory was New England, especially the Boston area, meaning he had to travel often to notions stores that sold Streamline products and make sure the displays were all in order. The company's motto, plastered on billboards and appearing in the *New York Post*, was "DAZZLE the Missus with Spiffy Rhinestone Buttons from STREAMLINE."

Artem took his job seriously. He was determined to make a good living, to impress both his boss and his father-in-law, who still called him a putz—meaning a fool in Yiddish—when he thought Artem was out of earshot.

CHAPTER NINE

While away on sales calls, Artem started to think that his family might be happier and better off in New England. He knew a family who had packed it all in to move all the way to Rockland, Maine, where the father opened a drapery store. He could do this too, he thought. Yet he knew nothing about draperies and in any event would need substantial capital to open and sustain a business.

How could he get quick capital? Artem wondered. Raising money buying cartons of cigarettes or booze in North Carolina and selling them in the neighborhood was a possibility, but not at the level he would need to start or buy a business. If he started earning additional funds on the street, he would be bald by the time he had saved enough money, he thought. Asking his father-in-law for the money was out of the question, even if Artem promised to pay it back, because his father-in-law would be constantly hounding him about how the business was doing and when Artem would be able to repay him.

Always the schemer, Artem figured out how to pull a rabbit out of the hat. He had almost forgotten about the diamond-and-emerald earrings he had taken with him from *Andrea*

Doria and kept with his baseball card collection in a shoebox in the bedroom closet. The shoebox was dusty when he opened it. There were the earrings, bright as the day he had grabbed and pocketed them!

When he had arrived back in New York aboard *Stockholm*, he had entertained the possibility of finding Ruth Roman and returning the earrings. Yet he kept doubting whether that was the right thing to do. If he kept them, Ruth Roman would never find out. She might have been reimbursed by insurance for their loss, and if not, that was her problem, not his. He might as well keep the jewels for a rainy day, he had thought.

Artem looked out the window and saw the pounding rain. "Oh my god," he exclaimed to himself. "This is that rainy day. I'll sell the earrings and buy a business!"

He had to broach the notion of moving delicately and couldn't mention the earrings to Sylvia. So slowly, over the next few weeks, he brought up how much he liked New England and asked if she would consider moving. At first, she was skeptical, but after a while she started to like the idea. The Boston area had large Jewish communities, she realized, and she and Artem would feel right at home in any of them. "But what would you do to support us?" she asked.

"I could buy a business!"

"And where, exactly, would we get the money to buy that business?" Sylvia asked. Deep down, she feared that Artem might bring up the possibility of borrowing a generous sum from her parents. That was a nonstarter for Sylvia because she didn't want to appear greedy or dependent.

"I have received a letter from a lawyer saying that my Uncle Harry in Chicago recently died and has named me in his will as a beneficiary. I don't know how much I'll get, but it should be substantial."

"Who the hell is Uncle Harry?" asked Sylvia. "I never heard you mention him, even when we were preparing the guest list for our wedding. Why is that?"

"Because our family and his were never close," said Artem without missing a beat. "I was as surprised as you when I heard that he had left me money in his will."

"Why didn't you tell me this before?" Sylvia asked.

"Because I just got the letter yesterday and don't know how much money I will inherit. I didn't want to get your hopes up."

"Well," Sylvia said, "I guess that changes things. I trust you, and if you think we can swing it, I'm OK with the idea."

The next day was Friday, and Artem didn't need to go into the office until the afternoon, when he planned to log the button orders from his recent trip to Boston. On the way, he stopped in the Diamond District on 47th Street. At 15 West 47th Street, he took the elevator to the fourth floor and entered a glass door engraved with the name "Edelstein & Sons Jewelers." The receptionist asked if he had an appointment, and he said no, he was there to speak to his uncle, Stuart Edelstein. Hearing Artem's voice, Stuart came out from the back and greeted Artem with a big hug. "How long has it been, and what brings you here?" asked Stuart.

"It's been too long, and I'm here because I need some professional advice," Artem responded.

"I have with me a certain pair of earrings," Artem continued. "These were entrusted to my care by my wife's grandmother, who needs money and wants to sell them. She asked me confidentially if I could help her out because she doesn't want anyone in the family to learn what she is doing."

"Let's take a look," Stuart said.

Artem then dug into his right pocket and retrieved a carefully wrapped package, which he opened and placed on the jewelry pad on the counter. "Oh my," Stuart exclaimed, "these are exquisite! Each sapphire must be at least eight carats. And the diamonds...I'm not sure I have seen that many on one piece of jewelry except maybe on the Crown Jewels at the Tower of London.

"Do you think you can help me sell them?" Artem asked.

"I think I can," Stuart said. "Give me a few minutes to think about this." Stuart's first step was to examine the earrings closely with a jeweler's magnifying lens. Doing that confirmed that they were of perfect quality and near-perfect clarity. He couldn't determine the weight of the diamonds without more analysis but estimated that it had to be at least twenty carats in total.

Artem took a single Hershey's Kiss from the bowl on the counter and unwrapped it. He put it in his mouth and slowly sucked on it while Stuart was thinking. He was in no hurry, and Kisses were his favorite candy.

"One option would be for you or me to take these to Sotheby's or Christie's and see if it would be willing to accept them for auction," Stuart offered. "One problem with that is the length of time it would take. The earrings would need to be appraised, and the chain of ownership might be examined. Once the amount of the opening bid is established, they will have to be included as a lot in a future auction, which will be advertised to the public. The timeline is lengthy. Another problem is that commissions are high. Either Sotheby's or Christie's will deduct a seller's commission from the auction proceeds, probably in the vicinity of 10 percent of the hammer price."

"What's a hammer price?" Artem asked.

"It's the final price of the item, determined when the auctioneer bangs his gavel and declares the item sold.

"A second option would be for me to shop these around," Stuart said, "and see what I can get for them. But you should consider whether Grandma would want you to do that," Stuart continued. "It will only draw attention to the fact that she is selling her jewelry. If it becomes widely known, it may raise adverse inferences. Others may assume that she needs the money, which, based on what you have said, I suppose she does. I would advise that you talk to her before going down that road.

"Yet another option," continued Stuart, "would be for me to buy them from you and put them in the safe for now. I could consider how best to dispose of them. I might decide to break them up into individual gems and sell them piecemeal. Or I might decide to hold on to them and wait for the market to go up. It has been flat for the past few years and is bound to improve at some point."

"Do you have an estimate how much they might be worth?" Artem asked.

"I'd say between $150,000 and $200,000," Stuart said. "I can give you a cool $75,000 right now if you're interested."

Artem waited about half a second before he said, "Deal." Stuart wrote out a check for $75,000, which Artem asked to be in his own name. Stuart asked why, and Artem told him that his wife's grandmother didn't get out much and it would be easier if he handled the finances and deposited it in Grandma's bank account for her. Trusting Artem and knowing how important even distant family members are to Jews, Stuart acquiesced. Artem snatched the check, left Stuart's store, and proceeded directly to the Greenwich Savings Bank on Broadway, where he deposited it.

CHAPTER TEN

Deciding where to move took Artem and Sylvia several more months. They settled on Gloucester, Massachusetts, because Artem liked the area and Sylvia had heard there was a nice synagogue there. Artem loved the water and wondered whether the area might have some sort of marine-related business to acquire. He examined the classifieds in the *Gloucester Times* and found a charter fishing company for sale. It sounded perfect: a going business with two fishing trawlers. Artem didn't have any kind of commercial vessel license, but he was sure he could obtain one after the right instruction. One problem was the owner wanted $100,000. Artem offered $75,000, and the owner countered at $95,000, his best and final offer. Artem said he would agree to pay $100,000 if the owner would accept $75,000 in cash now and take back a loan for the remaining $25,000. The owner said he could accept that structure, and the two agreed on a term of fifteen years for the loan, adjusted annually at prevailing interest rates. So Artem bought the business contingent on the existing, aging owner staying on for a transition period while Artem went to Power Squadron School and obtained the necessary commercial fishing licenses. By the end of September 1959, the family had moved to Gloucester. Artem had become the proud owner and proprietor of Gloucester Sea Charter Outfitters.

Initially, the business had three charter vessels. Over the next decade or so, Artem expanded the number to ten, with the help of loan guarantees he was able to obtain under US government financing programs.

Artem had purchased the business with the idea that it would be easy to run and become lucrative. He shortly figured out that was not the case. It was lucrative but hardly easy. Artem had to put in long hours with the boats, as well as at home with the company's financial books. There was a lot of staff turnover, and each time someone was hired, Artem needed to train the new employee, which was exceedingly time-consuming. And the weather itself caused challenges. If high winds, large swells, or a storm were forecast, he would have to cancel charters, all the while paying employees and refunding deposits. Moreover, unexpected storms, including nor'easters, were not uncommon. How could he ever forget the Ash Wednesday storm in March 1962, which devastated the mid-Atlantic? It wasn't forecast to hit New England especially hard, and Artem was a neophyte mariner with too much confidence, so he readily took a group of fishermen into the Atlantic in one of his boats in search of tuna. The wind was not that forceful, but the swells were easily twenty feet. The boat bobbed up and down through the swells. He, the crew, and the passengers thought they were going to end up in the drink, or perhaps canned along with the tuna. Only with the providence of God were they able to make it back to Gloucester Harbor.

While in Gloucester, Sylvia had two more sons. All three attended the Fuller School, O'Malley Middle School, and Gloucester High School. They also received schooling in the ways of the sea.

When he was sixteen, the eldest son, Mark, started to spend summers working in the family business. At first, he would greet the charter customers on the dock, help them on board, serve drinks, and then hop off the boat, spending the rest of the day in the office answering phones. When the boats returned, he would help with the catch and then wash down the deck and cockpit, scrubbing hard on his hands and knees.

Eventually Mark obtained his captain's license, which opened the world to him, proverbially speaking. During summers, while home from the University of Vermont, where he studied business and learned the skills of outdoor survival, he captained some of the charter trips and earned good money in the process. Having a captain's license also immeasurably improved his social life. The insurance policy for the boats required that a licensed captain be on board whenever a boat was under power. Under normal circumstances, Mark might have successfully implored his dad to overlook this requirement. But Mark knew not to ask, because the boats were valuable financial assets that his dad could not afford to lose.

Once he secured his captain's license, Mark began to invite his friends to join him on evening sails. Each charter would return to the dock around 3:00 p.m., after which the boat would be cleaned. Mark's guests would arrive around 6:00 p.m., bringing beer, gin, and vodka with mixers, and sometimes dope. As the host, Mark would provide sandwiches and dessert treats from Virgilio's, a local bakery. At 6:15, Mark would cast off, steer the boat to Wingaersheek Beach, and drop anchor. For several hours, the guests would enjoy the libations and one another's company in whatever ways seemed most appropriate.

While probably not kosher in all respects, these gatherings were at least under the radar. On July 4, 1967, all that changed. About 8:00 p.m., as everyone sat quietly aboard *Sassy Lady*, a smaller boat approached from the distance. Mark thought it was going at too high a speed and seemed to be on a collision course. He jumped up and immediately started to flash the running lights. He then turned on the boat's powerful strobe and repeatedly sounded the pneumatic horn. At the last minute, the other boat spotted *Sassy Lady* and veered hard to port in an attempt to avoid a collision. But it was to no avail. The bow of the other boat, *Dream Queen*, rammed into the starboard side of *Sassy Lady* at a speed of about ten knots. The resulting hole fortunately was well above *Sassy Lady*'s waterline.

People on both vessels were tossed in all directions and suffered minor injuries. Multiple individuals on nearby anchored boats phoned the Gloucester Harbor Patrol, which immediately dispatched several boats to the scene. The officers administered first aid and took several people from both boats to the hospital for evaluation and treatment. Fortunately, no one was seriously injured. Because *Sassy Lady* was at anchor and the driver of *Dream Queen* was intoxicated, the collision subsequently was found to be the clear fault of *Dream Queen*.

This was small comfort to Mark, whose parents were apoplectic. Artem told Mark he was grounded for a month and would have to pay back the damages over time from his salary.

"What salary?" Mark asked, in his typically surly way.

"The salary you will be making working for me at the marina," Artem responded. "And you will be earning only minimum wage."

So Mark became a regular running charter trips and doing scut work at the marina.

One of Mark's regular charter customers during his late high school years was the Meserve family from Marblehead. Percy Meserve, the patriarch, had made his money running booze to the Boston Irish during Prohibition. Several generations later, Randall Mellon led the hugely successful family investment business from his office in Boston.

Mark never knew who from the family would show up, but it was usually three or four of them, sometimes cousins from different branches of the family. His favorite was Lucinda, a diva in her early twenties who had the body of an angel. Often, she would bring her younger brother Dan. Sometimes it would be her cousin Ralph or his sister Andrea. Whenever Lucinda was there, she invariably was sporting a skimpy halter top and string bikini bottom. She would smile at Mark and ask if he wouldn't mind rubbing suntan lotion onto her back before they cast off. He always would pretend it was an effort but, in the end, would accommodate her. When out in the Atlantic, she liked to sit on deck all the way up in the bow so she could feel the waves to the maximum. Each time the bow lifted on a wave, it felt like sitting on a rollercoaster going up into the sky. When the bow fell from the crest of a wave, it felt like jumping off a cliff attached to a bungee rope.

When the Meserves were out on the water with Mark, he felt like he could relax and be himself. It didn't matter to them whether they caught any fish, or if he decided to crack open a can of beer. From time to time, Lucinda would act flirtatious toward Mark, and he would dish it right back. Once Lucinda suggested that Mark visit her at the family home in Marblehead. Her family was having a clambake, she said, and it would be fun to hang out. He thought about it for a moment before declining. He would have loved to go but thought the party was bound to be another source of trouble for him. He didn't want to end up drunk and boisterous. He didn't want other people talking about him, especially those in the Marblehead crowd who might be a source of future customers. He wouldn't have minded if Lucinda invited him upstairs for some private time but sure as hell didn't want to take the risk of being caught by Mrs. Meserve in flagrante with her daughter.

CHAPTER ELEVEN

A rtem, Sylvia, and their boys led a charmed life in Gloucester. They first rented and later bought a small New England colonial in Gloucester's Magnolia section, a small town of its own on the water, adjoining Manchester-by-the-Sea. Immediately after moving there, they joined the oldest synagogue, which had been founded in 1904 by Jewish families in the Cape Ann area, which consisted of Gloucester and surrounding communities. The Jewish population wasn't large, but it was close knit, and Sylvia wasted no time making new friends and hosting Shabbat dinners. She also promoted herself within the congregation as the unofficial wise woman whom anyone troubled about anything could come to for advice. On many mornings, after the boys had left for school and Artem was at the marina, people would show up at her house unannounced. She always invited them in and offered them coffee and a delectable to eat. Often it was homemade rugelach, apricot hamantaschen, or a slice of mandel bread.

Usually, the conversations were largely mundane. June Abramowitz wanted Sylvia's thoughts on how old her daughter needed to be before she was allowed to date. Harriet Glazer wanted advice on how to handle finding cigarettes and condoms in her sixteen-year-old son's dresser drawer. Barbara Stein wanted to talk about how the temple planned to enforce the rules for the upcoming confirmation weekend retreat, where girls were supposed to sleep on one level of the hotel and the boys on another. Things got a bit thorny when Phyllis Shaffer took Sylvia aside to say she thought Ruth Mankowitz was having an affair with the rabbi. The claim subsequently proved to be true after Phyllis' teenage son, Ben, found a pair of red panties in the back of the rabbi's car on a ride home from the retreat. Ben stashed them in his backpack and subsequently handed them over to his mother, who noticed the name "Ruth" embroidered elegantly in the inner lining. Phyllis immediately called Sylvia to divulge the new evidence and to crow that she had been right about the rabbi. Sylvia told the president of the temple, who promptly convened an emergency meeting of the board of directors. The board called in the rabbi, who at first denied doing anything wrong but eventually confessed. Deciding that even rabbis need to be held accountable, the board fired the rabbi for conduct unbefitting a man of his office and stature.

For his part, Artem carefully honed his persona to establish himself as a respected member of the business community. He joined the local Rotary Club, where he made many friends. Eventually, he was offered a position on the membership committee, which he covetously accepted. Always on the lookout for new types of community outreach, he recommended that the club sponsor the annual Blessing of the Fleet parade and a partial college scholarship for a business-oriented high school senior. He helped build the club float for the annual Independence Day parade. Each year, he and his brothers walked proudly in front of the float, right behind the firefighters with bright yellow hats, wooden axes, and a Dalmatian. Largely because of his efforts, Rotary Club membership increased by 200 percent over a ten-year period. In 1982, for his efforts, he was awarded the Rotary Club man-of-the-year trophy, which stood sixteen inches high and bore the likeness of Gloucester's Eastern Point Lighthouse. He displayed the trophy proudly on the fireplace mantle. Guests often commented on it, and when they did, he was quick to mention that it was four inches taller than the annual trophy awarded by the Gloucester bowling club to its highest average scorer.

Artem was frequently quoted in the *Gloucester Daily Times*. He knew the associate editor from the temple men's group and used that connection whenever he possibly could. In summer 1976, Gloucester hosted an armada of tall ships traveling around the United States to fete the US bicentennial. It had been in New York City over the Fourth of July, traveled to Boston, and then spent two nights in Gloucester on its way to Camden, Maine. The City of Gloucester was hosting a clambake in the harbor to welcome the sailors. Everyone who was anyone was there, from the mayor to the city manager on down. Artem set up a beer stand at his boat dock, offering red Solo cups brimming with Sam Adams draft to anyone who wanted them. And somehow, Artem was clever enough to figure out how to induce his friend to publish a boxed notice in the weekend edition reading "Enjoy a glass of stout at the clambake compliments of Artem Finberg if you are over twenty-one and resolute enough to handle it." It ended with the aphorism "He who does not go in search of the things he truly wants is not truly a man. And man oh man, you should want this beer."

Years later, after a developer had chopped down more than two hundred trees to make way for sixty new homes on an old, foreclosed estate, he penned and secured publication of a short story taking aim at the three zoning commissioners who had approved the project. Entitled "Fairy Tales in Gloucester," it noted that "three local stooges in charge of land use planning had felled Snow White's forest to build mighty McMansions for themselves and other elites on land on which Robin Hood and his Merry Men had frolicked for centuries, doing good deeds for the community." It was a little embarrassing when, a month later, the president of Artem's synagogue signed the first contract to purchase a house in the new development. Five years later, Artem bought a house in the same development. Those who knew him could only shrug and say it was not surprising.

In business, Artem was known for being hard as nails. His primary goal was to expand his fleet of vessels. Fortunately, he could rely on the Federal Ship Financing Program to obtain 87.5 percent financing at favorable rates from the Federal Financing Bank, an agency of the US Department of the Treasury. He regularly obtained new loans by submitting the reams of financial documents required by government regulations. By treating certain long-term debts as off-book obligations, he was able to pass the financial tests with flying colors.

At work at the marina, however, Artem was known as affable and easygoing. He was all smiles when boat customers arrived, offering them free cold sodas and water bottles. They would go out with one of his captains for an afternoon or the day, returning to shore marveling at the wonderful time had by all. Artem, in turn, would give each of the guests a big hug, urging them to come back soon.

Although Jewish, Artem used the Christmas holidays as a business development opportunity. Late December was typically when business fell off for the winter season, so Artem had more time on his hands. Each year around that time, he would have month-by-month calendars printed for the following year, with a photograph of a different Gloucester scene for each month, and then would mail them to all his customers and those he thought might be customer material. When he did so, his kitchen would be a disaster, with piles of calendars everywhere while Sylvia addressed all the envelopes before taking them to the post office. Also, Artem would place a Christmas tree at the marina and decorate it with miniature lobster pots and white tinsel strands. When someone commented about the oddity of his celebrating Christmas, he would point out, indignantly, that this was a Hanukkah bush, not a Christmas tree, and that the speaker in any event should keep his big mouth shut.

One aspect of Artem's personality that made him stand above many other individuals was his genuine concern about people less fortunate than himself. He was one of the first individuals in the Gloucester area to participate in the Toys for Tots program around the holidays, and he was instrumental in persuading his synagogue to participate. While he was doing well in business and his family had no financial concerns, many in the Gloucester area were not so lucky. The fishing industry was the major employer in the area, and workers in the industry were not especially well paid. The area had a low median income. Also, fishing employment dropped at holiday time, meaning that many families had less disposable income to buy presents for their kids. Artem's Toys for Tots efforts were a genuine source of joy for many of the area's young kids. When Sylvia would complain about all the time he was spending away from home collecting toys and kids' clothing, he would just glare at her and ask, "Where's your compassion?"

Even though Rachel and I belonged to the same synagogue as Artem and Sylvia, which we joined when our kids were little, we did not know them. We would nod in passing at Rosh Hashanah and Yom Kippur services, but that was about it. We were not deeply religious, and neither were our kids. Nor were we temple elites like the Finbergs.

Often, when Sylvia spoke to her father, he would ask how the business was going. "Very well," she would say. But she never had a true sense of things. Artem would often buy her nice things, like the gold bracelet with a few diamonds he purchased for her fortieth birthday from his uncle in the New York Diamond District. Artem had saved up some money and thought Sylvia deserved a nice gift, so he called Uncle Stuart and said he wanted something a bit showy for Sylvia so her friends at the synagogue would be envious, but not so ostentatious that it would raise eyebrows around town and suspicions as to how Artem might have been able to afford such a bauble. "I think I have just the thing," Uncle Stuart said. "A fellow came in here last week saying his wife had become sick with cancer and he needed money for the treatments, so he was reluctantly offering to sell me the bracelet his wife had smuggled from Germany in a hidden compartment of her suitcase when she escaped to London on the Kindertransport in 1938. The bracelet had been a gift to his wife's mother, Berte, when she graduated from gymnasium in Munich, shortly before Berte and her remaining family members were transported to Dachau. It was a simple flat band made of eighteen-karat solid gold, with a total of six small diamonds spaced roughly two inches apart, according to Stuart. "Why don't I send it to you by insured mail and see if you like it? If you do, keep it, and send me a check. If you don't, just return it."

Artem said it sounded nice, but how much would he have to pay for it? "Let me think," said Stuart. "The man asked for $2,000, not knowing I would have appraised it for $4,000, but I told him I couldn't pay him anything close to that amount. I offered him $400 and said I would totally understand if he wanted to go elsewhere. He asked if I would give him $500 for it, which I did, and I'll let you have it at cost. A veritable bargain, I'd say."

Artem said he would like to buy the bracelet, and it arrived a week later, just three days before Sylvia's birthday. Fortunately, Sylvia wasn't home when it arrived, and he ripped open the wrapping. It was exquisite, he thought when he saw it. The gold had been polished, and the diamonds had been cleaned, so they sparkled in the light. Artem thought Sylvia would love it. He was quite pleased with himself until he looked inside and saw there was an inscription: "Gretchen, Mögen deine Wünsche im Leben alle in Erfüllung gehen." Aghast, he just stared at the inside of the bracelet. I wonder what that means, he first thought. Then came the worry that Sylvia might never wear something secondhand, except possibly something coming from her own family.

Not one to wait long before acting decisively, he picked up the phone and called Uncle Stuart. As soon as Stuart answered, he blurted, "You didn't tell me the bracelet had an inscription!"

"Good afternoon to you too," Stuart responded. "I didn't tell you because you didn't ask, and frankly I forgot about it. It is no big deal. Lots of estate jewelry pieces have inscriptions."

Artem took a deep before breath before asking, "Do you know what the inscription means?"

"I don't because I don't remember what it says. I do remember it was in German."

"Let me try to read it to you," Artem said. "'Mögen deine Wünsche im Leben alle in Erfüllung gehen.'"

"Oh, that means "May your wishes in life all come true."

"Can you just grind off the inscription?" Artem asked.

"Absolutely not. The bracelet is thin as it is. If I take off the inscription, it will fall apart. Perhaps you could tell Sylvia this is an old piece with a potent inscription meant for someone else but likewise applying to her. You can joke that her first wish—a good husband—has already come true."

"An interesting idea," Artem said. "I'll think about it."

He did, and that was the approach he took, although he decided not to tell Sylvia that the first woman who had received it later perished in the Holocaust. When Sylvia was given the bracelet, she was absolutely thrilled. She put it on immediately and showed it off to all her friends on the synagogue's social committee.

CHAPTER TWELVE

Contrary to the expectations of some people, running a New England business that involves fishing is extremely challenging. The commercial fishing industry and others wishing to fish must take seasonality into account. While skate, monkfish, and haddock are prevalent all year, swordfish and yellow tuna are available to catch only in the fall. Bay scallops and sea urchins are fished in the winter, bluefish and porgy are fished in the spring, and black sea bass, dogfish, and bluefish are fished in the summer.[6]

Another consideration, for commercial fishermen, at least, is the price of the catch, which can vary considerably in accordance with supply and demand. Overfishing can create a real problem. For instance, in the 1990s, according to the US National Science Foundation, "Atlantic cod populations fell to 1% of historical levels, due to decades of overfishing. Starting in the 1970s, powerful trawlers equipped with advanced radar and sonar systems allowed commercial fishermen to collect cod from a larger area and fish more deeply and for longer periods than ever before."[7]

Perhaps the factor making things most problematic and arduous for all fishermen, including charter fishing companies like Gloucester Sea Charter Outfitters, is the weather. With fishing off New England taking place throughout the year, storms and sudden weather changes make fishing difficult and unpredictable, especially during the winter. Danger lurks everywhere and all the time. According to one journalistic source:

> Since colonists first started taking their nets out to sea in Gloucester, more than 10,000 fishermen on the job from that city's port and at least 3,000 more from the New Bedford and Fairhaven ports have lost their lives since 1900. Those numbers don't include other smaller working ports along the coast in Boston, Hyannis, Scituate, and Plymouth as well as Nantucket and Martha's Vineyard, where the legacy of fishing is a family tradition.[8]

From time to time over the years, hurricanes and tropical storms devastated the area. There was the Great New England Hurricane of 1938, Hurricanes Carol and Edna in 1954, and Hurricane Bob in August 1991. Probably most notable for Gloucester, however, was the so-called Perfect Storm, which slammed Gloucester in late October 1991 and lasted for several days. It got its name from the fact that it was produced by the collision of three separate weather systems—a Great Lakes storm system moving east, a Canadian cold front moving south, and Hurricane Grace moving northeast into the North

Atlantic. When the three systems intersected in an extraordinarily rare meteorological event, they produced weather conditions of biblical proportions, including the hundred-foot waves that sank the *Andrea Gail* and caused the demise of all six of its crew members.

By the time the Perfect Storm occurred, Artem had become hardened by the ferocity of New England storms. Even he, however, couldn't ignore the impact that this meteorological explosion had on his community. After the ten-day search for the *Andrea Gail* was called off and the ship was declared lost, Artem headed straight for the Crow's Nest, a waterfront bar owned by the family of Bob Shatford, one of the crew members on board the *Andrea Gail* when it went down. He ordered his usual Sam Adams, raised his glass to those present, and made a toast to the vessel's crew and all other fishermen lost in the area over the years. Artem repeated the process every November for the remainder of his life.

CHAPTER THIRTEEN

Small for my age until college, I was never athletic and certainly not part of the "in" crowd. But I did have a certain sense of pride that carried me through situations and set me apart from others. When I was ten, I went on a birthday outing to a nearby amusement park with a bunch of neighborhood kids. Everyone wanted to ride the bumper cars and ran immediately to the gate. I was mortified because I was too short to get in, even craning my neck as high as I could in a vain effort to reach the height line. The birthday boy's father saved the day by whispering that the two of us could ride the Ferris wheel together. This sounded like a good plan, and I actually enjoyed it, although I couldn't help but feel different from all the other boys. No one said a word to me about not riding the bumper cars. I told myself it wasn't my fault that I was short, and I tried hard to let go of the shame. But it was difficult.

The neighborhood in which I grew up consisted of several interlocking streets of split-level houses, built in the 1950s during the baby boom to accommodate upwardly mobile couples that wanted more space and grassy areas for their growing families. There were lots of kids around my age in my neighborhood. That was a blessing in many ways. You could always find someone who'd want to take a bike ride. The night before Halloween was called mischief night, because all the kids would run wild, throwing eggs at houses and toilet papering the trees. (Can you imagine if this were to happen today in Ahmaud Arbery's neighborhood?) On Halloween, the neighborhood was awash with groups of costumed hobos, ghosts, and princesses carrying milk cartons to collect pennies for UNICEF and shopping bags to hold gobs of candy. The leaves were falling around the same time, prompting many families to burn piles raked to the street and to roast marshmallows. In the spring and summer, everyone would run out the front door each day to buy ice cream popsicles when the Good Humor truck came by. Once each year in the summer, the fog truck would come by spraying clouds of DDT to kill the mosquitos. This created the opportunity for a unique form of entertainment—running after the truck to hide in the fog while ingesting the seemingly harmless chemicals.

This also was a time when the weekend's entertainment for parents was playing bridge while sipping Dewar's scotch and sharing news about mutual acquaintances (now called gossiping). And all the adults smoked cancer sticks! When my parents had dinner parties (which was often), everyone would light up during cocktails, creating a steely haze that was difficult to see through and perfect to cause fits of coughing. When those took place, I hid in my room and couldn't wait for the guests and the din of their loud voices to disappear.

Most days after school, the neighborhood kids would gather in the street to play baseball or football, depending on the season. My mother always encouraged me to go outside and join in, and sometimes I did, but this was because I felt I should, and I never had fun doing it. I always felt self-conscious and couldn't wait until darkness crept in and forced an end to the activities. In gym class at school, I was sometimes fine and sometimes not, depending on the sport being taught or played. Tennis was fine. Although I was not good at serving, I could at least move around a lot and hit the ball in a volley. Getting it over the net was a fifty-fifty proposition. Gymnastics was also iffy. The pommel horse was hard to master, but that was equally true for most of the other kids. I excelled at the ropes, usually making it all the way to the gym's top rafters. But again, baseball and football were the bane of my existence. When impromptu teams were formed, I usually was picked last, or next to last if I was lucky. I could feel the anxiety permeating me as I assumed my assigned position (usually left field in baseball and one of several wide receivers in football). In baseball, with luck, no one would hit the ball to left field. In football, the quarterback was unlikely to throw me the ball.

I am sure my mother felt she was doing the right thing when she kicked me in the pants, so to speak, and urged me to head outside, but it certainly didn't feel that way. In retrospect, I wish my father had taught me the best ways to throw and catch a baseball and football, but he was equally uncomfortable with those sports and probably had no desire to do that. I wish that, as I grew older, I had asked my parents to hire a trainer to help me bulk up, increasing my confidence, but I never even thought of the possibility. Using the metal chin-up bar in the doorframe of my room delivered a little bit of that confidence, but not nearly enough.

Fortuitously, I was a good student. I had to work hard to get good grades, but I did (often instead of sticking my toe into the social waters) and usually was able to get As. That was a confidence builder. But making good friends proved difficult. My closest childhood friend was Alec, someone I knew through sailing. We were in a yacht club junior sailing program together, racing fourteen-foot sailboats against others on Long Island Sound. At our urging, our fathers bought a larger boat together, and we raced that too. I felt like the imperfect one, but Alec must have had vulnerabilities and made at least a few mistakes. In the only mistake that I remember, he was at the helm of our boat during a race. It was windy, blowing around fifteen knots. We were on port tack, approaching another boat, which had the right of way. Alec thought we could pass in front of the other boat but at the last minute changed his mind. He pulled hard on the tiller in a doomed effort to veer to port and go behind the other boat. It didn't work. We crashed into the other boat, breaching its hull, and causing its wooden mast to splinter like a baseball bat. Fortunately, no one on either boat was injured.

Without realizing it, I thought of Alec as the brother I did not have. It felt as though we were all but related. Alec was the best man at my wedding. In my late-twenties and thirties, we began to move apart. I cannot say why with clarity, but I suspect my mother, Joan, unwittingly played a role. If she found it advantageous, desirable, or merely convenient, she would offer a bold opinion about almost any subject known to man.

Alec's wife, Nina, liked my mother's antics and stoked her ego. My mother showered love and attention on Nina and made it plain she wished I had married someone like her. Had I done so, I can only imagine what my life would have been like. Years later, after my friendship with Alec had faded, I learned that a neighbor had just attended a wedding at which she had met Alec, the father of the bride. Upon hearing that, I felt pangs of lament. I decided to send Alec an email congratulating him and expressing regret that we had drifted apart. In his reply email, Alec suggested that we get together in Boston during an upcoming trip he had planned. We reconnected, briefly but not meaningfully, and have not spoken in a long time. It saddens me to this day, but having pondered the subject, I now get it. Alec was more driven than I. He was an extrovert, and I was not. I was yearning for an emotional connection he neither felt nor desired.

On the surface, being adopted never seemed like a big deal. From early in my life, my parents read from a set of books provided by the adoption agency, called *The Adopted Family* and *The Family that Grew*, which tried to inculcate the idea that adopted babies are special and loved more than other babies. Unlike kids who lived with their biological parents, adoptees like me were "selected" from a vast baby pool. My parents (particularly my mother) often told me how much they adored me. No other parents could possibly love their own children more. My mother was blessed by God, and I was the perfect son. I would remain so forever—so long as I remained devoted.

It is hard to describe my mother adequately. Outwardly, she was gregarious and friendly. She also was judgmental. At home, protected by our four walls, she often would talk about people in hypercritical terms. Harold was a dimwit and wouldn't have amounted to much without his rich father-in-law, who set him up in business. Connie flaunted her wealth and her Jewishness, donning flamboyant jewelry and speaking with an affected (New York) accent. She adored Estelle, who had such a kind heart—but was overweight, always dressed in black, and wore too much makeup, thus looking a little freakish. When I was in high school, my mother's brother—my uncle—had an affair. I would have thought my mother's love for her brother might shine through, but I was wrong. She was furious with him and told his wife, Rita, to throw the bum out. Rita instead decided to repair her marriage.

My father loved me but was not as effusive. He also had his quirks. Undoubtedly insecure, he made a point of showing off to others. He proudly wore a set of eighteen-karat gold buttons on his blue blazer, pointing them out to others in the room. He also was born of expectations, which I experienced for the first time when Rachel didn't respond to him with the respect he thought he was owed. Because I could not control Rachel, I became a renegade son.

Looking back, I realize I measured my worth from my parents' reactions to things I did, not from an inner sense of self. Had my parents not adopted me, I would have been cast off at the side of the road. As I went through life, I had a never-diminishing hunger to unearth my biological past. Perhaps then I would take in what I already knew intellectually—that unworthiness was not the cause of my abandonment.

When I was in my late thirties, my great-aunt Tess died, and I helped my grandmother make the funeral arrangements. Riverside Funeral Home provided a limousine to collect us at my grandmother's apartment in New York and take us to the service. On the way there, we stopped to pick up my great-aunt Hanna, who was aghast to see me in the car. "What are you doing here?" she hollered venomously. "You were adopted—*You're not part of the family!* Get out of the car." It was such a ludicrous statement that I thought it was funny. I told her that her outburst was ridiculous and beyond the pale. Yet as I think back about the incident, I may have heard a whisper of truth in her words.

CHAPTER FOURTEEN

On the day after I turned thirty-four years old, my mother died suddenly of a heart attack. I suppose I shouldn't have been surprised because she smoked like a chimney and never believed in visiting doctors unless there was no other option. When she died, I was married, and we had our first daughter. At the time of my mother's death, my parents and I had many unresolved issues, which had gripped our family and metastasized. I had gone from being the perfect to the prodigal son.

The trouble, I believe, stemmed from the "sudden" (actually, it was not sudden) entry of Rachel into our family. My parents assumed incorrectly that the four of us would function as the three of us had before, with our family triangle becoming a quadrilateral and my parents reigning from the top. Rachel wanted nothing of this and happily (for her, if not for me) conveyed her views. Although I had tried to smooth things over between Rachel and my parents, I was utterly unsuccessful. My parents stopped phoning. I dreaded calling them because my mother would end up distraught and my father furious. Nothing I said would make a difference.

I was in Norfolk, Virginia, preparing for depositions on the day my mother died. Aware that I was going to be there that day, my father called Rachel and asked for the phone number at the office in which I was working. Rachel didn't know but said I had changed my plans and was going to stay overnight in Norfolk instead of flying home. She asked him what was wrong, and he wouldn't tell her. He wanted to speak only to me. Rachel said she would tell me to call him as soon as I called her later that evening. My father took a wild guess that I would stay at the same hotel in Norfolk where I had stayed on my last trip (he remembered the name), called that hotel, and reached me with the news. By then it was too late to get a flight back home, so I had to deal with my mother's death by myself in my hotel room, with Rachel by phone.

The funeral was the worst thing I had ever experienced. We were pariahs. My parents' friends shunned me. Almost two years later to the day, my father followed my mother to the grave. The funeral was a repeat of my mother's and excruciating. Yet afterward, I felt free to seek the truth about my ancestry.

Shortly after my mother died, my father gave me my adoption papers, which I hadn't known even existed. They showed I had been in foster care from birth to six months old and that my recorded birth name was Michael Eisen. Prior to that, I'd typically experienced a rush each time I heard the name Michael. Whenever I heard Peter, Paul and Mary singing "Michael Row the Boat Ashore," I felt an unexplainable inner warmth. Now aware of my birth name, I don't understand why my parents would have changed it. Did they love the name "Ishmael" so much that they were willing to overlook the potential emotional distress of changing my identity? They probably just thought I wouldn't know the difference, but that wasn't true.

CHAPTER FIFTEEN

Had I started searching for my biological roots and told my parents, they would have been distraught. No matter what I said, they would have thought I didn't love them. Now, that concern was a moot one.

New York State, where my adoption was finalized, had a strict law designed to prevent adoptees from finding their biological parents, and vice versa. The widely held view was that adoptees were in good placements with their adoptive parents and that upsetting the apple cart would not be helpful. It also was thought that allowing the sharing of information would tear apart adoptive families. None of this made sense to me.

With my birth identifier in my quiver, I placed my name in the New York State Adoption Registry. That enabled me to receive nonidentifying information about the adoption. I contacted Louise Wise Services, my adoption agency, and requested a written report. The response I received was formulaic, telling me that my birth mother was a twenty-year-old unmarried Jewish woman of Eastern European descent with no financial means to support a child. Her mother had died of cancer at a young age and her father had remarried the proverbial wicked stepmother, who had no interest in raising or even seeing her new husband's teenage child. The agency said it knew of no siblings of mine. It also revealed that my birth father was a man of Jewish descent in his mid-twenties, with three older brothers, also of Eastern European descent. His profession was listed as carpentry. The information was fascinating but incomplete. I still wanted to learn about my birth parents and their relatives, including my half siblings if I had any.

I regularly traveled to New York City on business trips. On one cold day in March, I detoured to the New York Public Library to search for birth records before heading home. I knew I had been born on Staten Island in New York City, and of course, I knew my birth date. I surmised that my birth mother would have been born in 1929 or 1930, so I searched the 1930 and 1940 censuses to see if I could find any females with the surname Eisen born in one of those years. I found Kayla, Muriel, and a handful of others. At the library I was able to cross-reference those names to women named Eisen who had given birth. None matched. I found an entry for one unidentified woman who'd had a son on my birth date, and a birth registration number was there. I looked up that number in another book and found only what I already knew—that the name of the boy was Michael Eisen.

It was discouraging to leave the New York Public Library empty-handed. Yet I knew I could keep trying to find other leads and that a bill was pending in the New York Assembly to unseal the state's adoption records. Perhaps I'd get lucky, and the bill would eventually be enacted into law.

As the years marched on, I felt less and less urgency to find my birth mother. However, the subject of my adoption never left my mind. One day in 2006, my wife and I were strolling down Broadway in Manhattan, where our daughter Jocelyn then lived, and saw a man coming toward us. I stopped in my tracks, thinking he bore an uncanny resemblance to me. The man stopped too. That conceivably could have been a turning point for me. Could he possibly have been a biological brother or relative? I will never know because I took the easy way out and continued to walk on.

CHAPTER SIXTEEN

Rachel and I have two daughters, Amy and Jocelyn. Because my own name is so uncommon and sometimes feels like a barrier, we spent a fair amount of time and effort coming up with names for both of them.

We both liked the name Jocelyn, but Rachel wanted to name the first child after her late grandmother, Agnes. In the Jewish tradition, naming a child after a dead relative is considered a mitzvah. The name doesn't have to be identical—it merely needs to begin with the same alphabetical letter. Fortunately, using the name Agnes was a nonstarter for both of us. We quickly decided on Andrew as our name for a boy. For a girl, we finally settled on Amy.

Based on the stories Rachel told, Agnes sounded as though she had been a sweet soul. As a teen, whenever Rachel wanted to go on an outing with her nana, Agnes would drop everything to make it happen. A particular treat for Rachel was going into the city on a shopping expedition. Often, Rachel would ride her bike to her grandparents' and propose the idea by shouting "Shopping trip time!" Upon hearing this, Agnes would run to the hall table to collect her bag and white gloves and to ring the brass bell to summon the chauffeur, who would pull the Cadillac out in front. Before being dropped off on the Upper East Side to sift through the racks of the latest fashions at Saks Fifth Avenue, Bergdorf's, and Bonwit Teller, Agnes and Rachel would lunch at the 21 Club or Sardi's. Afterward, if Rachel hankered for a black-and-white cookie, they would stop at the Stage Deli.

Amy and our second child, Jocelyn, were both solid students, but Jocelyn had more intellectual curiosity, and their personalities were distinctive. In her formative years, Jocelyn loved to sit in her room and read books. Amy was far more gregarious, preferring to cruise the mall in search of boys than to sit in the stacks at Borders. She was a star forward on the high school soccer team.

Toward the end of high school, Amy gave Rachel and me a real run for our money. It was not uncommon for her to tell us a white lie. I vividly remember the evening in 1994, during her senior year, when she said she and her friend Mattie were both going to Hillary's for a sleepover. Rachel asked if Hillary's parents were going to be home. Amy rolled her eyes and said, "Of course, Mom. I know your rules and wouldn't think of breaking them. No liquor. No drugs. No boys. Be back at Hillary's by 11:00 p.m. if you have gone out with your friends. And most of all, the sleepover must be chaperoned."

"That's right, sweetie," Rachel said. I might have been a little more lenient but had learned long before that Rachel and I needed to put up a united front. Prior to that, the typical situation was that Amy would ask Rachel for permission to do something, Rachel would say no, and then Amy would come to me and pose the same question. I was the softie and would usually say OK.

On that evening, Rachel received a call from her father saying, in a stoic voice, that her mother had just collapsed at home. The EMTs were there and there was no pulse. There was nothing they could do. She was gone.

Rachel talked for a minute about what had happened and decided we needed to tell the girls. Jocelyn was upstairs doing homework, so we both headed up together and knocked gingerly on the door. Jocelyn looked at us quizzically.

"We just got a call from Grandpa Cal," I said. "Unfortunately, I have some bad news. Grammy collapsed at home a little while ago. The EMTs came, but it was too late. She didn't make it."

"Oh, wow," Jocelyn said, "I'm so sorry. Do you think it is OK if I call Grandpa? I would like to tell him I feel bad."

"Of course," I said. "I'm sure he would love to hear from you."

Rachel and I then realized we needed to tell Amy. I picked up the phone and dialed Hillary's number, which Rachel had made Amy leave on the pad before she left for the night. It rang three times, and then came the familiar click of the answering machine, followed by a sonorous message announcing that the Martins were not home and directing the caller to leave a message after the tone. I thought it best not to leave a message, so I hung up and redialed. Again, the phone rang three times, followed by the familiar click. So I waited ten minutes and tried again. Still no answer.

After about five attempts, I decided we ought to go over to Hillary's house to tell Amy. It was only a ten-minute drive.

Hillary lived in a beautiful white colonial at the end of a long, windy driveway. We were about to turn into the driveway when I noticed the flashing lights near the house. A police car was there, and two uniformed policemen were standing in front. I saw several boys running out the back door through a neighbor's yard toward the adjoining street. Rachel asked one of the officers what had happened, and he said not to worry. It was just a high school party getting out of hand—incredibly loud, so one of the neighbors had called the police.

"Where are the parents?" Rachel asked.

"Out of town for the weekend."

That abruptly ended the conversation. We walked inside, saw Amy, and told her she needed to come home with us. The ride was not pleasant. There were lots of tears and lots of excuses. Amy had had no idea there was going to be a party or that Hillary's parents would be away for the weekend, she said. Even today, I'm not sure whether I believe her.

Fortunately, things seemed to turn around somewhat quickly. Amy was accepted by multiple colleges and ended up going to Bates, where she majored in English and again excelled on the soccer team. She made lifelong friends and now lives in New York with her husband, a doctor.

Our younger daughter, Jocelyn, followed in my footsteps and attended Williams College, nestled in the Purple Valley of northwestern Massachusetts, where it snows all winter, making the nearby Berkshire Mountains "dreamlike on account of [all] that frostin'."[9] Jocelyn majored in psychology and minored in French, reading Rousseau, Zola, and Proust without translation. I was proud.

For me, Williams had been the almost perfect college choice. Because it was in a beautiful mountain setting, I was able to learn to ski in a PE elective. A midweek ski pass at nearby Brodie Mountain was cheap, and I went skiing many afternoons in the winter after class. The January "winter study" session was a time to take only one course, and on a pass-fail basis, which allowed time to decompress with friends. This was a time to explore potential areas of interest—either on campus or off. One of my friends learned celestial navigation while sailing in the Caribbean. One of the best things about Williams was that it had abolished fraternities six years before my arrival as a freshman. The fraternity houses had been transformed into residential houses, with similar social activities but none of the pressure to pledge and the risk of rejection. Additionally, the academic courses were top notch. The professors were true teachers, first and foremost, and most classes were small.

Jocelyn also loved Williams, but her experiences were different from mine. I was there during the time the college (like many other men's colleges) was beginning to accept women. When Jocelyn attended, it was a full-fledged coed school. Jocelyn was also part of the theater crowd, playing minor roles in college productions and even staying in Williamstown after her freshman year to participate in the Williamstown Theatre Festival. She loved being part of the close-knit acting community. She also never liked the snowy winters the way I had but tolerated them because of the other things that Williams had to offer.

In 1999, during her sophomore year, Jocelyn said that she wanted to go abroad the following year. She chose Paris because of its colorful history and beautiful architecture. The baguettes, pastries, and wine weren't a bad draw either.

"Do you want to go first or second semester?" I asked.

"Definitely second semester, because that's when all my friends are going abroad." Susan and Katie were going to Australia then. Becky was going to Italy. And Kit would be in Washington, DC, doing research at NIH.

I'm sure that avoiding the frigid January nights in Williamstown also was a motivator.

Jocelyn ended up studying at the Sorbonne and living nearby in a rented room of a women's home on the Rue du Bac in the nearby Seventh Arrondissement.

I had added an international calling feature to our AT&T phone account. Mobile phones were just starting to be used in Europe, and Jocelyn was able to buy one in France that had a feature allowing international calls. Both plans had ridiculously low rates for calls at off-peak times, so communications back and forth were easy and cheap. It cost less to call Paris from Boston, and Boston from Paris, than it cost to call New York City. So we were able to imagine Jocelyn's life vicariously. She was enjoying classes and being invited to plenty of parties at classmates' apartments on the Left Bank. She often met friends at bistros in the evening. Île de la Cité was only a stone's throw away (actually, a brisk walk), and she regularly went to evening concerts at Sainte-Chappelle, above the crypt where Marie Antoinette was confined to contemplate her sins prior to being beheaded.

One Saturday in May, Jocelyn phoned to say she was going away for the weekend with a guy she had met at the Sorbonne.

He was American, she reported, but was in Paris on the Butler University program. As far as Rachel and I knew, Jocelyn was not the partying type and had never had a long-term boyfriend. So I had concerns but didn't want to give her the third degree. Rachel, however, had other ideas.

"Sweetie," Rachel asked, "what's this guy's name, and how well do you know him?"

"His name is Matt, and he's so sweet. We met at a bar on the Boulevard Saint-Michel, a local hangout for students our age."

"Where does he go to school in the States, and what is he studying?"

"He goes to Stanford and is studying French, of course. We all are."

"Well, I mean, what is he majoring in?"

"Oh, philosophy. He can wax poetic about Kant and Kierkegaard for hours over a bottle of Vouvray, our favorite type of white wine from the Loire Valley. In fact, that's where we are heading for the weekend—the Loire Valley, that is. Matt found this great old château converted to a hotel."

"Where is it, and what's it called? I wonder if we've been there."

"It's called Domaine de la Tortinière in Montbazon."

"It doesn't ring a bell, but I'm sure it's nice."

"Oh, yes. It's on acres of land with a swimming pool, not that we expect to use it. And our room is in the turret of the château."

"It sounds lovely," Rachel said. "I suppose I shouldn't bring up the sleeping arrangements."

"Oh, Mom, absolutely not," Jocelyn said. Changing the subject, she said, "We plan to see Chenonceau, Chambord, and Cheverny, and also to meander through Amboise."

"Our favorite was the Château du Beauregard," I threw in for no specific reason.

Three days later, I was sitting on the back deck when our phone rang. It was Jocelyn, telling us that she had had a wonderful weekend. She and Matt had gotten close and were starting to call each other boyfriend and girlfriend.

"That's so nice," I said. "I'm so happy for you and can't wait to meet him."

As fate might have it, I had the opportunity six months later, when I was called to Paris to work on a submission for the government of France in a maritime case in which France was a party. I asked Rachel if she wanted to come too, and she responded with an emphatic "Of course."

The case was before the International Tribunal for the Law of the Sea (the "Tribunal"), established to adjudicate disputes under the United Nations Convention on the Law of the Sea (the "Convention"). Finalized in 1982, the Convention set territorial limits of member states in the world's seas and established a legal framework for the use and protection of the seas, including all marine and maritime activities. The case on which I was working was called the *Monte Confurco* case (Seychelles v. France). The *Monte Confurco* was a fishing vessel owned by a company registered in the Seychelles and flying the flag of the Seychelles. In November 2000, the vessel was operating in the exclusive economic zone of the Kerguelen Islands in the French Southern and Antarctic Territories. At 23:25 hours on

November 8, 2000, it was boarded and seized by French authorities, and its captain was arrested. The vessel was charged with illegally fishing in French territorial waters, and a French court subsequently required the posting of a bond of 56.4 million French francs ("FF"), roughly US$9.4 million, as a condition of the vessel's release. The Seychelles filed a complaint at the Tribunal seeking an order reducing the amount of the bond and immediate release of the captain. Much of my work was on justifying the amount of the bond based on the value of the fish and the vessel. Unfortunately for France, the following month the Tribunal ordered a reduction of the bond to FF 18 million and immediate release of the captain. I was lucky, however, because I had the opportunity to visit with Jocelyn and try out several new Parisian restaurants.

We first spent time with Jocelyn alone, who wouldn't stop waxing eloquent about Matt. "He is my soul mate," she said. "He's smart, witty, and good looking too." He had been in the military before enrolling at Stanford and thus was a few years older, but "that just means he is more mature." His family lived in Hillsborough, California, she told us, but had a ranch in Montana, where he'd learned to ride horses and rope cattle. We wanted to be happy for Jocelyn, who had never had a long-term relationship. But Rachel and I both had a nagging suspicion that this might be too good to be true.

We met Matt one evening with Jocelyn at a highly recommended bistro called La Fontaine de Mars, near the Eiffel Tower. Later made famous by a visit of the Obamas, it was not well known at the time. The tables were adorned with bright red-and-white checked tablecloths and bustled with an endearing vibrancy found only in Paris. The maître d' led us up a narrow flight of stairs to the second floor and into a room we were told would be comfortable and quiet. We were soon disappointed, finding that the table of eight next to us was occupied by a noisy group of friends from Pittsburgh, whom we quickly named the "Ugly Americans." But the bottle of wine we ordered drowned out some of the noise as we waited for Jocelyn and Matt's arrival.

Jocelyn came in first, giving Rachel a peck on the cheek and me a big hug. Then, with great fanfare, she said, "Mom and Dad, this is Matt. Matt, these are my parents."

The food at La Fontaine de Mars was delicious and the evening was quite enjoyable. Matt seemed serious with a slightly mischievous side, and he clearly liked Jocelyn. During the meal, Matt told us a lot about himself and his family. His parents were members of the St. Francis Yacht Club in San Francisco, he said, which was where he'd learned to sail. He had spent several summers with his aunt in Locust Valley, New York, and been a sailing instructor at the nearby Sea Cliff Yacht Club on Long Island, where, coincidentally, I also had taught sailing some thirty years earlier. Matt said he was planning to go to law school eventually but for the moment was content to be a student in Paris. I asked Matt what had prompted him to study philosophy, and he responded with what struck me as a glib answer: "It has enhanced my critical thinking skills and hopefully will be useful in future problem-solving." For some reason, I chose to believe him.

After returning to the United States, Jocelyn and Matt continued to date during their senior year. During the several weekends that he visited, Jocelyn would refer to Matt as her Stanford Tree (the Stanford mascot) and Matt would refer to her as his Purple Cow (the Williams mascot) with a prominent udder. That was a bit sickening to hear. The thing that bothered me more, however, was that they couldn't keep their hands off each another. I pulled Jocelyn aside once and told her to please try to tone it down, and she didn't respond very well, saying that I needed to remember that I had been young once myself and probably acted the same way. "Oh, no, not in front of Grandma Joan," I said. She would have told me how improper it was to behave that way and that I'd better stop if I wanted her and my father to keep paying for my education.

"The Dreyer family is above that nonsense, and you're a member of that family," she probably would have said. I can remember reminding my mother that my father used to brag about having sex with many willing girls when he was sixteen years old and her slapping me hard across the face in response, saying that those dalliances were of no concern to her; *she* was a virgin when she got married.

After three years of dating, Jocelyn told us that she and Matt were going to move in together. She had a well-paying job in advertising, and he had a good job on Wall Street, or so he said. Each of them had been living in a separate apartment with roommates, and they found a large one-bedroom in a new-ish building on West 69th Street, right near Lincoln Center. The area had lots of dogs and reasonably priced restaurants. Rachel and I would occasionally take the train to New York and spend the weekend seeing them while staying on East 50th Street at the Benjamin. At first, the living arrangements seemed to be working well. Eventually, Jocelyn told us that Matt had been spending late evenings at the office and occasionally had to go away on business for several days at a time. She trusted him. On a cold day in November 2003, Jocelyn found a Ritz-Carlton hotel keycard in the outside jacket pocket of the suit he wore home. She confronted Matt, and he brushed it off, saying that it must have been from his recent trip to Chicago. He hoped it would be the end of the matter, and it was for a while. One day when he was out of town, she retrieved an envelope from the mailbox addressed to a man named Jason Mitchell. She opened it, thinking it must have been to a former tenant. At first, she surmised that it was. A notice of tax assessment from the Internal Revenue Service, it was demanding the payment of back taxes, interest, and penalties in the amount of $243,033.67. Jocelyn was mulling what to do with it when she noticed a cautionary statement at the bottom: "If you are not Jason Mitchell and your Social Security number is not 487-55-2490, you are required by the Internal Revenue Code to respond to this notice by contacting the IRS immediately." That Social Security number appeared vaguely familiar. After a few minutes, Jocelyn remembered seeing that number on a bank statement addressed to Matt. Matt's real name must be Jason Mitchell.

When Matt arrived home that evening, Jocelyn casually mentioned that she had opened an IRS notice, thinking it was addressed to one of them.

"I was actually quite relieved when I noticed it was addressed to someone else," she said, "because the person owes over $200,000."

"What a relief," Matt responded. "That's a lot of money."

"Aren't you curious who the fellow is?"

"Not really—but OK, what is his name?"

"Jason Mitchell. Have you ever heard of him?"

Matt took a big gulp but held his composure, saying, "The name doesn't ring a bell. Perhaps he used to live in this apartment."

"Are you sure you don't recognize that name? If not, maybe you recognize his Social Security number. It's 487-55-2840."

No, Matt responded, he didn't recognize that number either.

"I do," Jocelyn said. "When I first saw it, I realized it seemed familiar. The light slowly came on, and I remembered seeing it in one of the recent letters to you from Citibank. You are Jason Mitchell, aren't you?"

"No, no, no, you must be mistaken about the whole thing. My Social Security number is similar."

"What is it, then?"

"Oh, it's…458-77-1956."

"I wish I could believe you, but I don't. Show me a document with that number on it."

The jig was up. The two just looked at each other for what was probably only thirty seconds but felt like an hour.

"Let's sit down and talk," said Matt. They sat facing each other on the love seat, which wasn't emitting much love at that moment. And then, like water from a fire hydrant that has been unscrewed, it all came pouring out.

"Babe, I suppose I have something to tell you," Matt began after uttering a loud sign. "My real name is Jason Mitchell, and that IRS notice is for me. I had thought that if I called my-self by another name, my creditors would not catch up to me. Now, I see the IRS apparently has.

"This started right after I returned to California from Paris. I didn't know what I wanted to do in life. My brother, Steve, suggested I take time off senior year to see if I could find my bearings. I had some savings, but not a lot, and told Steve I was skeptical about being able to support myself."

"Why don't you just rely on your credit cards?" Steve then asked. "Which ones do you have?"

Matt said he had two Visa cards and a MasterCard.

"What's your limit on those?" Steve then asked. Matt had responded that it was $15,000 on each Visa card and $18,000 on the MasterCard. Steve then commented that those lines of credit could take Matt a long way, especially if he were to pay only the minimums each month and walk away at the end, perhaps declaring bankruptcy if necessary.

"I told Steve I didn't want to declare bankruptcy but was intrigued by the idea of just skipping town once I was ap-proaching the borrowing maximum," Matt said.

"So while you were living on your own away from school, you intended to defraud the credit card companies," Jocelyn said to Matt, not so much as a question but as a statement of fact.

"Oh no," Matt said, "that's not right. Although I had little money of my own, I figured I'd get a job and earn a salary. I expected to pay the interest each month from that salary and to allow the outstanding balance to accumulate. Eventually, I would have figured out a way to pay it back." Then, after a long pause, he added, "Or declared bankruptcy, I guess."

"Sounds like fraud to me," Jocelyn said. "And you haven't talked about the fact that you also owe money to the IRS and lied to me about your name! You probably were never even enrolled at Stanford. I thought I knew you, but obviously, I don't. I want you to get out of my sight."

That night, Matt slept on the couch in the living room. As he headed to the bathroom the next morning, he engaged Jocelyn and tried to apologize. She wouldn't have it. "I want you out of here by the weekend," she told him. And never a pushover, Jocelyn meant every word she said. At 6:00 a.m. on Saturday, Matt walked out the apartment door carrying a large suitcase and a duffel bag stuffed to the gills with his belongings.

Matt had no idea where he was heading. He couldn't get past the feeling of rage at Jocelyn for being unwilling to give him a second chance. He headed toward his friend's co-op on 84th between Columbus and Amsterdam, hoping he'd be home and would provide a couch on which Matt could crash for at least a couple of days.

I was a late sleeper on weekends, and Jocelyn was always thoughtful about not wanting to wake me up. Promptly at 9:00 a.m., the phone rang. I was alone at home and cringed when I saw Jocelyn's name on the caller ID. She never called that early unless something was terribly wrong. When she did, my self-appointed role was to talk her off of the proverbial ledge.

For instance, Jocelyn once called from college during her sophomore year, sobbing hysterically, after having failed her macroeconomics midterm. My first thought was to wonder how anyone could fail macroeconomics; it's so much easier than microeconomics, I recalled. But then Jocelyn explained that she had studied hard and thought she knew the material. There had been no quizzes or tests of any kind prior to the midterm, and she hadn't realized what she didn't know. Now she knew. The professor had asked her to stay behind after class ended to talk about the test results. Rather than suggest that she come in for help or do extra work to help raise her grade, he told her that even if she aced the final, she would get no higher than a C- in the class. So the professor urged her to drop the class instead. She wouldn't get any credits, but at least her grade wouldn't count against her GPA. "Oh my God" was one of Jocelyn's favorite, or at least most frequent, expressions. She used it many times on the phone that morning. "Oh my God! Oh my God! Oh my God! What am I going to do?"

I told her in as soft a voice as I could muster to calm down. This was not the end of the world. No one was dying. She could take an extra course the following semester (not her first choice because of the added stress) or a class at a local university over the summer. Then I had a better idea. "Having your semester grade determined by a single test seems awfully unfair," I said. "Why don't you go see the chairman of the Economics Department during his office hours and discuss this with him? At least when I was at Williams, the top priority of professors was to support the students, and I doubt that has changed." Jocelyn liked the idea and went in to see the department chairman the next day. He was sympathetic to her plight and told her he would make sure she could take a makeup exam, but first he wanted to assign a senior economics major to act as her tutor. That was what he did.

I am still not sure Jocelyn is comfortable talking about the incident, but it proved to be a learning experience for problem-solving. The only real consequence was that Jocelyn decided not to major in economics, which she had been thinking of doing. The world is better off. She majored in psychology and became a clinical psychologist, which I think is far closer to her true calling.

On the fateful Saturday morning after Jocelyn kicked Matt out, I heard the same type of fear and uncertainty in her voice. Had she done the right thing? Or should she have given him another chance? She loved him but no longer trusted him. Did she have the requisite emotional IQ even to make an informed decision about her life? She wanted to find the love of her life; would she ever discover him? If she didn't, she would be lonely; how could she cope? With a final "Oh my God," Jocelyn verbalized that next month's rent was coming due and Matt probably wouldn't pay his half.

All I could do was verbalize the obvious. "You're in plenty of good company having to confront that kind of problem," I said. "Don't second-guess yourself." Then, "You've identified significant red flags, and it's good that you caught them early rather than into the marriage. You'll find someone you love even more," I added, with a tinge of guilt as I couldn't say that was absolutely true.

But I could say with certainty that Jocelyn was resilient and would bounce back from this setback. I also quipped, "If you turn thirty and are still unmarried, you can always apply to be a contestant on *The Bachelor*, although I suppose being selected as the bachelorette would be even better." She chuckled.

Jocelyn remained single for many years, meeting nice guys and some jerks on various dating apps. She finally met a great guy at a work conference in San Antonio and decided he was the one.

CHAPTER SEVENTEEN

Although Gloucester had a distinctly New England flavor, it was like any other town in America in many respects. Its government focused on addressing local problems, such as ever-increasing teacher shortages, student smoking of marijuana behind the high school, and pressure by some parents to expunge certain books from the school curriculum and town library. Gloucester had long prided itself as a bastion of New England free thought, offering high school English electives on Ralph Waldo Emerson and the American Transcendentalists, Mark Twain, Virginia Wolff, and Tennessee Williams. But controversies arose because some thought Emerson extolled individual actions over the greater good, Twain's novel *Huckleberry Finn* contained the n-word, and Virginia Wolff and Tennessee Williams both led proudly gay lifestyles. "We must vigilantly shelter our beloved children from the world's evils and temptations," crowed one faith-based community leader.

Starting in the 1990s, illicit drug use began to dwarf even those societal worries. Methamphetamine, crack cocaine, and, eventually, heroin use became widespread, especially by the homeless community, kids on playgrounds after school, and even housewives who in the past would have been satisfied to down glasses of Chablis with one another while chatting about local educational issues and the like.

As drug use was increasing, Artem and Sylvia Finberg's second son, Ricky, was in his midtwenties. Always an intellectual and free thinker, he had left Gloucester High in 1983 as a socially awkward kid bound for college at MIT in student-oriented Cambridge, Massachusetts. There, he excelled in his classes and graduated with an MS and eventually a PhD in electrical engineering. While in Cambridge, Ricky also expanded the scope of his pursuits, eating with friends at Durgin-Park, smoking some dope, becoming a Red Sox fan, hacking some websites (if not at MIT, then where?), and, perhaps most importantly, losing his virginity to a stoned girl named Molly, whom he met while listening to music at the Middle East on Brookline Street.

After graduating from MIT, Ricky took the straight-and-narrow path of looking for jobs at tech companies around Boston off Route 128. He landed one at AI Squared, which developed and produced "ZoomText" software used by visually impaired individuals to enlarge written text, change it from black on white to white on black, and convert it to audio. He felt amazingly good about himself. Not only was he earning a respectable salary, which enabled him to buy a brand-new red BMW convertible, but he also found satisfaction in the knowledge that his company was developing products designed to improve society.

While working at AI Squared, Ricky met a smoking chick named Emily Weld. Known to her friends as Emmy, she had long blond hair, wore little makeup (she didn't need it), and sported perky tits that peeked through her blouse like stars twinkling brightly in an undiscovered cosmos.

Emmy worked in the business development office. Even though she didn't have the same level of academic credentials, Ricky was determined to bring Emmy into his own universe. He invited her first for coffee, then for dinner, then for a few weekends away, and then, well, you know the rest. They became engaged on November 6, 1990, before Emily had even met Ricky's parents, or vice versa.

Emmy grew up with her sister, Carolyn, in a Boston Brahmin family on the exclusive flat side of Beacon Hill. She attended Emma Willard School and then Middlebury College. Her father, known to his Harvard buddies as Skip, was a past president of the Somerset Club, established in 1826 and the oldest of Boston's private clubs. The Harvard *Crimson* referred to the Somerset Club as "traditionally…the haughtiest and most prestigious of clubs," explaining that one does not reach out to join it but rather must be asked. Although the club did not accept woman until the 1980s, Skip's wife, Midge, was able to ingratiate herself with the members and their wives by running the club's annual charity auction and hosting weekend get-togethers at the family "cottage" on Nantucket Sound in Chatham.

Perhaps surprisingly, Skip and Midge were drawn to Ricky from the moment they met him. Although he didn't play golf, tennis, or squash, they could tell he was kind, funny, and perfect for their daughter. They thought they could mold him to fit into their lifestyle. Also, Ricky was smart, they knew, as evidenced by his degrees from MIT. Undoubtedly, he would have a solid career that allowed him to give Emily the material things in life to which she had become accustomed. At first, they were not thrilled that Ricky came from a Jewish family. Over time, that became less of an issue. The concern started to diminish when Skip and Midge realized they had met several nice Jewish people at the Somerset Club following termination of the club's WASP-only membership rule. The club had decided that the policy was limiting the size of the membership pool and, with it, the source of $100,000 initiation fees from new members.

Ricky and Emmy were married in the Welds' side garden in Chatham on July 9, 1992, at 5:00 p.m. in the afternoon. It was a beautiful Thursday, sunny and seventy-five degrees, with a ten-knot breeze coming in from the south off Nantucket Sound. Violet's Creative Catering of Cape Cod, unofficial caterers of the Kennedys, prepared exquisite food and libations, including a signature gin-based cocktail that they named "Emmy's Downfall." Music prior to and during the ceremony was provided by a small ensemble of flutes, violins, and a harp. As Emily walked down the aisle, flanked by her parents, the ensemble played Pachelbel's "Canon in D" instead of the traditional wedding march. A rabbi from the Finbergs' Gloucester synagogue and a reverend from the Welds' Episcopalian church jointly officiated. Ricky wore a blue pin-striped suit with a silver tie, which nicely complemented the tea-length white lace gown that Pricilla of Boston had designed for Emmy at Midge's request. After Ricky and Emily exchanged their vows, the guests noticed a dark cloud forming to the east and made a mad dash for the tents when the raindrops began to fall. Soon it was teeming, but the guests already had made it under cover. Thank goodness, because the Welds' guests would have looked like drowned rats rather than the high-society types suggested by their names. Ricky's parents and the guests from his side of the family were not similarly threatened with that affliction. All the women wore wide hats strewn with flowers, and the men had donned yarmulkes or strikingly high round fur hats, called "shtreimels," which extended over the ears and provided a modicum of weather protection.

At the reception, Ricky was approached by a guy named Griffin Carmichael, roughly Ricky's six-foot height and age. The resemblance between the two of them, however, ended there. Griffin had large muscles and was wearing a tight shirt that showed them off. His hair was dirty blond, which contrasted nicely with his sapphire-blue eyes. He usually wore a wide smile, which had cemented his reputation as a chick magnet in the country-club circuit. Ricky had short, curly, dark black hair and a trim, sculpted figure, which made him look like a golf caddy at one of the several clubs to which he belonged.

Griffin stuck out his hand to Ricky and said, "Hi, I'm Griff, Emily's cousin. First, let me congratulate you. Emmy is a great girl. I'm sure you and she will be blissfully happy. Also, I feel like I know you already. Maybe we could have lunch sometime." Almost like magic, Griff then whipped a business card from his jacket and thrust it toward Ricky.

"Why not," said Ricky as he pocketed the card. Only later did he look at it and see the strange reference: "Griffin Entertainment: We Cater to All Tastes." Quite an odd card, to be sure, Ricky thought. It contained no address or email, just a phone number: (617) 438-3673. Ricky had to admit that he was intrigued and figured he would follow up at some point.

Just as Griff was leaving, Emmy came over and gave Ricky a peck on the cheek, which made him almost forget all about the previous conversation.

"Your mother wants to start the hora," she said.

"Won't your parents go nuts?" he asked.

"Not if you give them a heads-up and tell them it is a nice American Jewish tradition," she said. He didn't have the heart to tell her that it is danced at Jewish weddings throughout the world, from Ashkelon, Israel, to Azerbaijan (at least by the small number of Jews still there). So Ricky looked for and found Midge and told her about the Jewish line dance his parents wanted to organize, which he said she might find fun. Never having seen the hora danced before, she stayed quiet for a minute, mulling over whether participating in such an event would offend her Boston Brahmin sensibilities. Eventually, without anything concrete to go on, she decided that it would not. She muttered, "Hell yes," holding a glass of Emmy's Downfall in her dainty right hand. It was her fourth of the evening.

The band started to play "Hava Nagila," and all the Finbergs' friends and family began to line up. Mark and his three cousins, Justin, Stu, and Solly, collected two felt-covered folding chairs, told Ricky and Emmy to sit on them, and raised the stunning couple above the crowd for all to see. They then bounced up and down, twirling the couple as the line dance encircled them.

"What a beautiful spectacle," screeched Sylvia.

"Oh my, what a peculiar ritual," Midge exclaimed as the photographers zoomed in on the smiling couple.

CHAPTER EIGHTEEN

Three and one-half weeks after the wedding, after Ricky and Emmy had returned from their honeymoon in the South of France (a gift from Emmy's parents), Ricky's phone rang at AI Squared. He usually waited for the third ring to see who was calling before answering. This time for some reason he just picked it up and heard, "Hi, Ricky—it's Griff here… Remember me from the wedding?"

"Of course," Ricky said. "It was nice to meet you there."

"That was a hell of a shindig you guys threw," Griff said. "I loved the stuffed clams and the oysters Rockefeller. And the surf-and-turf entree was marvelous."

"Glad you liked them," Ricky responded almost by rote. "The filets came from Savenor's in Boston, and the lobster tails were taken fresh off the boat in Rockland, Maine. But you must be used to parties like that, given the pedigree of your family."

"Actually, I'm not," Griff said a little sheepishly. "My mother and Midge are sisters, and Midge is the one who married into money. The girls grew up in a working-class family in

Lynn. I lived there too, with my mom and dad, who now runs the family hardware store.

"Your little party in Chatham ended up providing some nice late-night entertainment," Griff added. "I went to the wedding alone and met this sweet little thing dancing, and wow was she smashed. At first, she wouldn't tell me her name—only that she was also a cousin of Emmy's." Griffin said he quickly ascertained that she was related to Emmy distantly on the Weld side, not on his own side of the family. "After a couple of dances and a few more drinks, I learned that her name was Nancy and she had just finished her junior year at Amherst, which, as you may know, has a reputation as a party school. Nancy said she does shots and downs drinks until well past midnight every Wednesday through Sunday while at Amherst. Mondays and Tuesdays are dedicated to her studies. When I asked if she felt drunk at the moment, she avoided the question, telling me she couldn't remember how many Emmy's Downfalls she had consumed but that it didn't matter because she was having a good time."

Griff then lowered his voice, almost conspiratorially. "Guess where we headed after the last dance, buddy boy?" he said. "To the Chatham Bars Inn—we were lucky to get the last room. The only problem was the uptight older couple in the room next door, who called the front desk at two in the morning to complain that strange noises coming from our room were preventing them from getting their rest.

"Anyway, that's not why I called," Griff continued. "I'd like to see if we can grab lunch someday soon, like I mentioned at the wedding. My treat."

Ricky wasn't particularly sanguine with the things Griff had been saying, but he was still intrigued by the card he had been handed at the wedding. So Ricky responded, "Why not?" At Griffin's suggestion, they met a week later at a steakhouse in Lexington, close to where Ricky worked.

Griff started the conversation colloquially. "I hear you went to MIT—very impressive. I bet you had to work your ass off."

"I won't lie," Ricky said. "It was tough going at first. I had confidence I could handle the work but knew that the entire class was smart. I sort of freaked out and called home virtually every day, looking for encouragement. My parents provided it, telling me I was a smart kid who could hold my own. I'm not sure my mother believed it, but my father sure did. He was always the best at providing reinforcement, although not so much at showing emotion to his kids. But that's an aside. By the end of the first semester, I had done well in some tests and felt confident about the materials. I aced most of the semester finals."

"I wish I could say the same," said Griff. "But the truth is that I skidded through public high school with so-so grades. I spent a second senior year at Andover, rowing crew. I got into Dartmouth primarily because of my rowing skills, I believe. Likewise, it didn't hurt that Uncle Skip made a hefty donation to Dartmouth on my behalf, even though he himself went to Harvard. He also paid my Dartmouth tuition.

"I was a star oarsman at Dartmouth, but just an average student. I eked out a B-minus average, which was good enough to get me a job at State Street Bank, where I now work.

"Dartmouth was a wonderful place," Griff continued, "both for networking and as a source of datable women." The twinkle in Griff's eye sent the clear message that "datable" meant "easily beddable." "I met lots of cool kids from the best of families, and I am still in touch with many of them. Many of them like the finer things in life."

"I can only imagine," Ricky said in a flat, almost sultry voice, "but why are you telling me all this?"

"Because it's a nice segue to the main purpose of this meeting. I'm sure you're a nice enough guy, but I have a business proposition."

Ricky thought about the "Griffin Entertainment" reference on the business card and was beginning to feel a bit squeamish. He took a big gulp of his beer and said, "Let's have it." Griffin didn't disappoint.

"As I said, I work at State Street. I have a good job there, and it pays the bills for my condo in South Boston. But I want more than that, so I have a little gig on the side. Sometimes my friends from Dartmouth, or their friends, want help procuring services that I am in a position to arrange. Some may want companions for the evening, especially when their spouses are out of town. Others may want to enjoy certain substances that I can obtain. They wouldn't want to head to street corners for these and know that calls to me at State Street are above suspicion. Hell, if their phone records were checked, it would seem downright odd for there to be no calls to a highly reputable Boston bank."

"So are you suggesting that I send potential customers to you?" Ricky said. "I don't know many people of that ilk. Plus,

I wouldn't want to involve myself in the process of linking friends to illicit activities, even if they are inclined to engage in those activities on their own."

"Hell no, buddy," Griff said. "I have plenty of customers. I also have plenty of supply. What I don't have is a steady form of transportation. A few friends and I are starting a local distribution center to supply New England's needs. There are plenty of raw materials traveling by boat from South America to Canada and New England. We need a way to divert, or should I say *redirect*, some of them to us. Offer the boat captains enough of an incentive, and they will be more than happy to skim off some of the product and replace it with identically appearing bags of white powder. I know your father owns a charter boat company in Gloucester with multiple oceangoing vessels. I'd like you to help us use the vessels at night to pick up product at the rendezvous points and return it to us at shore points."

"And why would I do that?" Ricky asked.

"Because you'd be helping your dad increase his company's profits. And I would provide you with enough of a monetary incentive to make your eyes pop."

"No way. I don't need more money," Ricky said, "especially when it involves something that I assume is illegal. My salary at AI Squared is more than adequate. Also, as you know, my father-in-law, your uncle Skip, has plenty of resources and has been more than generous."

"You're going to find out that having a benefactor is not the same as having your own money. Say you want to buy that red Porsche 911 Turbo you undoubtedly have had your eye on. Are you going to ask Skip for the money to buy it? How about getting the money you'll need to spend a licentious weekend in Las Vegas with your buddies? And just wait until you start getting financial demands directly from your new wife!"

"You don't know me at all," Ricky said. "I'm not that kind of guy. Thanks for lunch, but I have a meeting I need to get back to attend. See you around."

CHAPTER NINETEEN

Although Ricky's marriage had started off well when he and Emmy were a pair of starry-eyed lovebirds, it did not go as planned. They ate out most nights because of their busy work schedules and ordered a nice bottle of wine with each meal. This, of course, added to the excitement of being a married couple and enhanced their time in the bedroom after they got home. But it also had a major adverse impact on their bank account. Once, when Emmy was meeting her father, Skip, alone for lunch, he ordered wine, and she commented that she and Ricky had been getting into the same habit for dinner. She also thought that was the perfect time to mention that that was getting expensive, so they might have to cut back. She fully expected her father to take a hundred-dollar bill out of his pocket and to hand it to her, with the comment that she and Ricky should enjoy themselves. She also expected him to say he'd be happy to give her more whenever she needed it. Instead, he said that cutting back on expenses was probably a good idea and that she and Ricky should start saving up for a house. He put the final nail in Emmy's proverbial coffin by telling her that he believed strongly that newly married couples should make it on their own—not expect or get used to handouts from a rich relative, even if the relative happened to be his or her father.

Emmy and Ricky in fact had been talking about buying a house. They had already saved some money from Ricky's salary at AI Squared—not enough yet for a down payment, but they were headed in the right direction. He mentioned seeing "For Sale" signs on some nice but modest houses off Route 128, which would be near his office. Emmy was lukewarm about the idea, preferring a wealthier town in Middlesex County, such as Wellesley, Weston, or Winchester. When Emmy added that those towns would have better schools for their children, Ricky gulped and said, "Let's table this discussion."

As the marriage progressed, Emmy's appetite for fine things expanded to other areas. Before their first anniversary, Emmy told Ricky she would love a new watch for her present. She already had her grandmother's dressy watch with diamonds and a knock-around TAG Heuer, but she required something flashier to wear at work lunches and dinner at the club with her parents. She mentioned that a Rolex would be nice, but she didn't insist on it. Ricky joked and reminded Emmy that something made of paper is the traditional first-anniversary gift. She glared at him defiantly and said, "That's not funny. It reminds me of a college friend who expected an engagement ring from her boyfriend on Valentine's Day but received ski mittens," she added. "As you might expect, that guy is now toast."

So Ricky took Emmy's request to heart and contacted his dad's uncle Stuart to see what he might suggest. When he mentioned that Emmy wanted a Rolex, Uncle Stuart said that would set him back at least $5,000. Ricky's eyes almost popped out of his head. He asked Uncle Stuart what brands might be less expensive but still nice. Stuart recommended a Longines, which was also Swiss and had a good internal mechanism. Ricky said that sounded good and asked Uncle Stuart to send him a catalog. Ricky picked out a fashionable Longines with a steel case and band, a gold bezel, and some gold highlights, but it was otherwise unadorned. He paid about a tenth of what the Rolex would have cost.

On the morning of their anniversary, Emmy ripped open the beautifully wrapped package. "Oh my, how lovely," she exclaimed, but Ricky could tell immediately that she didn't like it. Well, too bad, he thought. I did my best, and I think it's classy. Emmy then handed Ricky a set of gold studs and a matching pair of cuff links for the many formal events she hoped they would be invited to attend. He thanked her but wasn't any more excited than she had been about the watch.

Ricky was beginning to have second thoughts about the marriage. Had he done the right thing? Had he thought everything through sufficiently? He had had no qualms about marrying Emmy because there was a definite spark and the two of them seemed so compatible. As he was tossing around these thoughts, nature intervened. Emmy announced she was pregnant. She was thrilled, and Ricky said he was too. He couldn't possibly bring up his qualms now. He would simply have to show joy about the baby. He did that at home, to his friends, and to both sets of would-be grandparents.

In the spring of 1994, with his two-year anniversary and childbirth approaching, Ricky pulled Griffin's card from the top drawer of his desk and stared at it. Emmy had just left for a five-day trip to the Canyon Ranch with several friends, as sort of a last hurrah before she became a mother. Should I do this? he wondered. But not for long. I don't have much of a choice, he thought. He then picked up the phone and called Griff, who answered immediately, announcing "Griffin Entertainment" to the caller.

"Hi Griff—this is Ricky Finberg. I'm sure you remember me." Then, after an awkward silence, "Let's meet."

It took Griff less than a second to respond without any fanfare. "Sure. At the marina. At the bar at the Lobster House at six o'clock."

They did meet later that day. Griff arrived fifteen minutes early and ordered a Sam Adams draft. He then sat there, sipping it and waiting. Always the professional, Ricky entered the bar exactly at six. He said hello to Griff and ordered a Sam Adams.

"Have a change of heart?" Griff asked.

"Not so much a change of heart as a change of perspective. After thinking this through, I decided that the added income would come in handy, and that the enterprise is fairly low risk. We'd need to paper this over with a legitimate commercial transaction. Let's talk about the terms."

"I like the way you think," Griff said. "What I need is access to one boat one night per week from 9:00 p.m. until 5:00 a.m. on a day of my choosing. How you sell that is up to you."

"OK, how about this?" Ricky asked. "First, you establish a corporation—you could call it New England Maritime Transit Services, Inc.—for the stated purpose of transporting catch between large fishing vessels in the Grand Banks and New

England ports. This would be an efficient way for large fishing trawlers to send fresh fish back to the mainland every day without having to weigh anchor and make the trip itself.

"Then, we hammer out a long-term charter contract, to be signed by you as president of the company and my dad as president of Gloucester Sea Charter Outfitters, containing the terms and conditions of the agreed-upon transportation services. Let's call it a logistics agreement—that term has zest. I could ask a lawyer I know to write it up.

"My idea is not foolproof. It takes two days to motor to the Grand Banks and two more days to return. If anyone asks what you are using our vessels for, you will need a plausible alternative response. I'll leave that up to you. As far as we are concerned, you are using our boat to retrieve small shipments of high-value goods from Canada-bound ships and take the goods to the US. You'll have to provide assurances in the contract that you have prepared all the necessary customs documents. Of course, you probably will conclude that you don't want to file the documents."

"That sounds like genius to me, buddy boy," said Griff. "Why don't you ask your friend to do that? My only requirement is exclusive use of a boat on a night of my choosing each week. You need to arrange for the captain and crew, and I and/ or someone I designate must be able to ride along on each voyage. That will protect you, since my guys will go aboard the fishing vessel and handle the transaction. You won't have any actual knowledge of what the trips are for."

"One thing I'll have to think about is staffing the trips," Ricky said. "We'll need only a captain on each boat if you or someone you select goes alone. I can't be the captain because Emmy would be suspicious, so I'll have to think about who I might get. But it shouldn't be a problem.

"There also is the question of how much compensation you pay Gloucester Sea Charter Outfitters for each trip. It must be enough to make this enterprise both profitable and salable to my father, but not so profitable as to make him suspicious. The company normally makes 25 percent above the cost of each charter, including the amortized value of the vessel and insurance. I'll figure out the out-of-pocket cost of each nighttime trip, including the cost of fuel and crew salaries. Then we'll add a 75 percent markup, if that's OK."

"It is," said Griff.

"And now to the hardest part—how much are you willing to pay me for making the arrangements?"

"I was thinking $25,000 per trip in cash. Does that meet your expectations?" asked Griff.

"I was thinking $35,000," said Ricky.

"How about we split the difference at $30,000?" asked Griff.

"That sounds fine," said Ricky.

"Having a written contract is nice," said Griff, "but let's also shake on the deal. In my world a handshake is far more binding than something in writing, meant to be enforced by a court. A handshake signifies a sacred commitment for all eternity. He who breaks the commitment is subject to the wrath of the gods. Do you understand?" asked Griff.

"I do," answered Ricky with more bravado than he felt.

Then they shook hands.

CHAPTER TWENTY

Griffin had never set up a company before, so he knew he needed a lawyer. He had seen television ads for Mansfield and Fine, which promised "to guard your back and always keep your legal needs in mind," so he called the firm and asked for Frank Mansfield. Frank spent a lot of time at the Boston Municipal Courthouse trolling for new clients, so Griff left a message with the receptionist. Frank called Griffin back that evening and said sure, he would put something together. Frank drafted a standard certificate of incorporation and, to create flexibility, company bylaws containing a broad statement of business purpose: "To facilitate the maritime transportation of persons, goods, and aquacultural products within the New England and international waters and to provide such related services as the board of directors shall determine to be in the Company's financial interest." Within days, New England Maritime Transit Services, Inc. was established.

Before Ricky did anything else, he had to convince his father, Artem, that he had come up with a good idea for the business. That wasn't so easy because Artem had a habit of thinking that Ricky's ideas were off the mark. There was the time he'd wanted to buy an ostrich farm and asked Artem if he could borrow $100,000. Artem asked to see Ricky's business plan, but Ricky didn't have one. So Artem said no to the loan, much to Ricky's chagrin. On another occasion, Ricky thought it would be a good idea to open a Ben and Jerry's franchise in Marblehead. It, too, would have required a $100,000 payment up front, substantial additional investment of funds for ice cream equipment and shop construction, a $25,000 annual franchise fee, and 3 percent of the revenues. Artem calculated that with sales increasing 10 percent each year, it would take Ricky twenty years to recover the investment. Artem said there was no way he was going to put even a dime into that.

But this idea was different, Ricky thought. It would be an expansion of his father's existing business, not a totally new venture. And it wouldn't require any upfront monetary outlays, except for fuel and salaries, which would be reimbursed shortly after each new boat trip.

So on one Sunday afternoon, Ricky told Emmy he was going to see his father. He didn't say why—just that Mark would be at his parents' house with yet another new girlfriend in tow, and he wanted to meet her. He drove into the driveway at 2:00 p.m., and his father came to the door, having heard Ricky's old Cutlass convertible roaring down the street.

"Dad, I need to talk to you about an idea I have for the business."

"Oy vey," said his father, without thinking. He nevertheless invited Ricky into the study to give his pitch.

Ricky told Artem he had met a guy in the business of "lightering" fish and goods between Gloucester and large offshore fishing vessels. "He needs small boats to use at night, and I told him we might be able to help. He will cover our costs and pay a sizable markup."

"How much of a markup?" Artem asked.

"Seventy-five percent."

"That sounds almost too good to be true," Artem said. "But I guess if he's willing to pay that, who am I to question it? You can never be too profitable." Artem gave Ricky the OK to negotiate the terms of the contract, subject, of course, to Artem's final sign-off.

Gloucester Sea Charter Outfitters had a standard charter contract, which it used for its one-day and multiple-day charters. But it was for a fixed price and didn't cover the terms that would be needed in this type of arrangement. So Ricky asked one of his AI colleagues if he could recommend a lawyer, and that guy said that, in fact, his wife's brother-in-law was a lawyer and probably could help out. The lawyer put together a contract with the terms that Ricky wanted: a per-trip fee of $131,250, covering all costs and the 75 percent markup, payable within five days following the completion of each trip; a guarantee of one trip per week on the night of the customer's choosing with at least forty-eight hours' advance notice; and no contract termination date, although either party could cancel with thirty days' advance written notice.

After the two lawyers had spent a week or so tweaking the wording, Griff and Artem signed the contract. Griff and Ricky met at the Lobster House the next day to clink their glasses of Sam Adams lager in celebration.

Ricky had thought he might propose that he and Griffin sign a separate brokerage agreement covering the $30,000 weekly side payment. In the agreement, Griffin could promise to pay Ricky (or a company set up by Ricky) a "commission" for arranging business between New England Maritime Transit and Gloucester Sea Charter Outfitters. That might give both Ricky and Griffin some legal cover if anyone ever questioned the true purpose of the $30,000 weekly payment. However, Ricky then realized that the payments would be in cash, with no tax reporting or withholding. That in and of itself would be suspicious, suggesting an illegal kickback. Also, $30,000 was 22.9 percent of $131,250, the weekly revenue that Global Charter Outfitters would be receiving from New England Maritime Transit. A commission of between 3 percent and 6 percent would be reasonable—not one of 22.9 percent. What first had seemed like a good idea turned out to be a terrible one, and Ricky immediately dropped it.

CHAPTER TWENTY-ONE

During 1993, things were looking up for political liberals like the Finbergs. Bill Clinton had been inaugurated president in January and had chosen an oldie, Fleetwood Mac's "Don't Stop" (which includes the lyrics, "Don't stop thinking about tomorrow") as his unofficial theme song. (Truth be told, I much preferred "Don't Stop Believing," released by Journey six years later.) Later that year, Janet Reno was sworn in as the first female US attorney general, and Ruth Bader Ginsberg took her place on the Supreme Court. The economy was doing well, and the unemployment rate dropped to 6.5 percent by the end of the year. With great help from President Clinton, the Oslo Accords were signed by Israeli prime minister Yitzhak Rabin and PLO leader Yasser Arafat, setting up a framework for Palestinian self-governance and eventually a two-state solution for the conflict in the Middle East.

That year also was major for Pablo Escobar, leader of one of the largest cocaine processing and distributing organizations in the world. Founder and leader of the Medellín cartel and dubbed the "king of cocaine," Escobar had started his smuggling activities from and through Colombia in 1976. Prior to that, he was part of a gang that sold tombstones, sandblasted off their inscriptions, and then resold them to those who couldn't afford or might not want to pay market prices. Some with warped minds might call Escobar a modern-day Robin Hood, as he used his vastly increasing wealth to rebuild Medellín's barrios, and he paid for construction of parks, football stadiums, hospitals, schools, and churches. However, because of his crimes, he also was targeted by the US and Colombian governments and in 1992 negotiated his surrender in return for a term of imprisonment in La Catedral, a private "prison" in which he enjoyed a bar, hot tub, and waterfall. Apparently finding these inadequate, Escobar escaped later that same year and died in a police shootout on December 2, 1993.

Everyone who had half a brain knew who Pablo Escobar was, and Ricky was no exception. Ricky assumed that Griff was somehow connected with the Escobar-led cartel but didn't know for sure and was certainly not about to ask. What you don't know won't hurt you, his mother always said. So he breezily prepared for the new arrangement as if everything were copasetic.

Sitting alone at night in his study, he would fantasize about the additional $1.5 million he would be bringing in each year. And it would be tax-free. With that amount, he could easily pay for Emmy's extravagant trips and tastes in clothes and for the baby's expenses. If truth be told, Ricky also was troubled by the suspicion that the money was coming from a ruthless drug lord who earned it by selling addictive products to US citizens. Yet those individuals wanted what they bought, right? Ricky was merely involved in an enterprise working to meet public demand. Also, sometimes he would allow his thoughts to wander to the question of how he might put leftover funds to good use, just as Pablo Escobar had done. Ricky wasn't religious but imagined the public praise he might be able to garner by building a new sanctuary at his parents' synagogue in Gloucester. He was not a brute like Escobar, Ricky reassured himself. Any moral comparison between the two men would be ridiculous.

CHAPTER TWENTY-TWO

Once Ricky set his mind to doing something, he did not waste time second-guessing his decision. Less than a week after his handshake with Griffin, he began the planning process.

First and foremost, he needed to figure out how to crew the boat on the night it would be used by Griff. Ricky couldn't do it, he knew, because Emmy would never put up with his being away from home. Not to mention that even if she let him go, she would give him the second degree when he returned. "Where were you? Who were you with? What were you doing? When are you doing this again?" He certainly couldn't tell her the truth, Ricky knew.

Ricky immediately thought about bringing his younger brother, Doron, into the enterprise. Doron was eight years younger than Ricky and far less intelligent. What Doron lacked in this department he made up for in street smarts. He was now twenty years old and in his second year of courses at Bunker Hill Community College. Like his older brothers, he had grown up around Gloucester Sea Charter Outfitters, learning the ways of the sea. By the time he was ten, he could tie a bowline and name the parts of a boat. By twelve, he was skippering boats in Gloucester Harbor. By fifteen, he was taking out charter customers on fishing expeditions under the supervision of his father or one of his older brothers.

When he was twelve, Doron figured out that he could win over his teachers and classmates by being outgoing but polite. Whenever he met someone new, he would don a cheeky grin and thrust out his hand, saying, "Nice to meet you." He was always big for his age, too, meaning he was a daunting presence when in the company of those needing intimidation. One time after school, he was talking to his bud Jared, who was kind of a nerd. Jared was holding his bicycle, a top-of-the-line Schwinn. A tall but scrawny classmate named Nate came over and pushed Jared, saying "Give me that bike." Jared said "No way" just as Nate was approaching with his fists clenched. Doron stepped in front of Jared and told Nate to get lost. He did.

When he started college, Doron moved from his parents' house to a group home in Lynn with one of his friends and four of his friend's friends. It was a run-down row house, with a sagging floor in the kitchen and mouse traps scattered about. The kitchen sink was usually full of dirty dishes, and empty beer cans adorned the kitchen table and counters, but it was home, and Doron loved being there. On weekends they often would have parties, which would attract undergraduate girls from Endicott, Emmanuel, and Simmons Colleges. Usually, one or two of them would decide to sleep over.

The Finberg sons were not close to one another, and Ricky had not seen Doron since Passover, when their mother had pressured them to come over for Seder. It was now a hot Sunday afternoon in August, so Ricky figured he would just take a chance and show up at Doron's house. Hearing loud music from inside, he knocked loudly on the door. Doron answered it in an undershirt and ripped shorts, with a beer can in one hand.

"Bro," Doron said to Ricky, "it's nice to see you. Come on into our humble abode. I'm kind of surprised to see you."

"Well, it was spur of the moment. I was thinking about you, little brother, and thought I'd stop by to see how you're doing."

"I'm doing fine," said Doron. "Enjoying life, working at Dad's this summer, taking out charter customers, flirting with daughters who are old enough—you know the drill."

"Indeed, I do."

"But you didn't come here just to talk about those times, am I right?"

"Indeed, you are, little brother," said Ricky. "Let's go inside and talk."

That is what they did.

"Did you know that Emmy is pregnant?" Ricky started out.

"No, I did not. Who's the father?" Doron asked.

"Very funny," Ricky countered. "She's in the first trimester, with six months or so to go."

"Congratulations. I guess that means I'm going to be an uncle!"

"That is true. And that is what brought me here. Not to tell you the good news but because I want to see if you'd be interested in a related financial proposition."

"Why are you even thinking about that?" Doron asked. "Your father-in-law is oozing money, and I'm sure Emmy has a trust fund of her own, am I right?"

"You are right that Emmy's father is loaded and that Emmy has a trust fund, but her father has shown no interest in sharing any of his money with us, or in approving trust fund payouts to Emmy. Emmy has expensive tastes, which I have been working hard to satisfy. Now that we are going to have another mouth to feed, I have decided I need to supplement my otherwise adequate income. And I could use your help."

Ricky proceeded to describe the plan to Doron, but in basic terms. "I've identified a guy who wants to hire Gloucester Sea Charter Outfitters boats during off hours to take merchandise to and from large fishing boats. The company will be nicely compensated. I'd like you to be the captain. The company will pay you for your extra hours. I'll supplement that with a weekly bonus of, say, $3,000. How does that sound?"

"Let me get this right. If I fit these overnight trips into my schedule, I'll be paid my normal hourly rate plus $3,000 on top of that."

"That's right. And the $3,000 will be tax-free because it will be in cash and a special arrangement between you and me."

"As Mom would say, something about that seems a bit off—it just doesn't sound kosher."

"It's perfectly fine, Doron. Don't worry about it. The guy needs one of our boats to transport merchandise and is willing to pay a premium for it. I had the contract drafted by a lawyer I know. It's completely legitimate. I worked out the arrangement, so I will receive extra compensation as part of the finder's fee. I want your help, and so I will give you some of that."

CHAPTER TWENTY-THREE

Before anyone knew, they were in business. Griff decided that the best night for the operation was Thursday, when most ships heading north would pass close to Gloucester. There also would be no local commercial fishing of striped bass and other prevalent species, which the State of Massachusetts limited to Mondays, Tuesdays, and Wednesdays.

Each Thursday afternoon, Doron would appear at the marina around 6:00 p.m. to say hello to the staff heading home after a full day's work and to make sure the boat selected for the evening run was properly outfitted. Usually he chose *Fishaholic*, a thirty-five-foot vessel with an inboard Yanmar engine with a turbo add-on for extra speed. He would top off the fuel tanks, check the running lights, and make sure the vessel had life jackets. You never knew when you might be stopped by the Harbor Patrol or Coast Guard, and you wanted to avoid being cited for some inane safety violation, which could lead to bad things. Equally, you needed to have a credible explanation for what you were doing out at sea so late in the day. For this purpose, Doron loaded a large container marked "emergency medical aid," filled with defibrillators, ventilators, and EpiPens, which he would say he was taking from Gloucester to a port in New Hampshire. If stopped on the return trip, he would say he'd picked up the supplies in New Hampshire and was in the process of taking them to Gloucester.

Things went well during the first several years of the arrangement. Griffin or one of his associates would show up at the dock precisely at 7:30 p.m., after the regular boat staff had left, so they didn't suspect a thing. On each trip, Griffin or his associate would bring a nondescript black backpack, which he kept tightly zipped and clutched in his hand. They would motor for about two hours until they were twelve nautical miles offshore, safely in international waters. Once there, they would shut off the engines and wait patiently for a larger ship to appear in the southern sky. When it got to the designated latitude and longitude, which Griffin determined before each trip, the larger ship would slow its speed to two knots and set off three flares. Doron would do as instructed, which was to shoot off two flares and then proceed to the ship. When close behind, Doron would pull the smaller boat alongside, and Griffin or his associate would move to the larger ship. After being on board for five minutes or so, he would return to the smaller boat with the same backpack clutched in his hands. The boat then would head back to Gloucester, another two-hour journey.

Doron didn't know what was in the backpack and only once made the mistake of asking. "That's a pretty small bag for such an elaborate operation as this," Doron mentioned to Griffin. "What's in the bag?"

"It's none of your business," Griffin answered. "If anybody asks, say nothing, or your own head will end up in it."

"Very funny," said Doron. "I know you have worked this out with Ricky and my dad, so I'll leave it at that."

The timing of the trip was perfect. The regular staff was gone when Doron started preparing the boat for the evening, and when he left it at 5:00 a.m., it looked exactly as it had when he had first boarded it. Doron was exhausted after each journey, but he could go home and sleep late the next morning, as he had arranged not to have any Friday classes. He worked at the marina each Saturday and Sunday. On Monday morning, he was ready for his next week of classes.

CHAPTER TWENTY-FOUR

Having to juggle the nighttime trip with classes and his weekend work was not an easy task. Doron did it cheerfully and banked a lot of the money he was making. He also found time for a fulfilling social life. On most weekends, he would sit through the parties held at his house, drinking beers with his friends, his roommates, and any others who would show up. That changed in 1994 when he met Amy.

Doron always knew he wasn't smart like Ricky, who had taken AP courses in high school before going to MIT. Doron was one of the "average" students; he had had gotten through high school with a solid B average in courses taken by all the jocks. World history was a bitch because you had to learn the names of all the European monarchs. It wasn't easy, but he had set his mind to it and ended up with a C+ after the grades were adjusted for the curve. He had liked some of the girls in his high school but never clicked with anyone special. Those smarter than he wanted nothing to do with him, and those in his classes seemed a little bit dull. Go figure, he once thought—the girls in my classes are attractive, but they don't talk about interesting things. I'm into current events and classic rock, and they are into cheerleading.

In February 1994, Jeff, one of his housemates, invited Doron to drive with him to Winter Carnival at Bates College in Lewiston, Maine. Maine had had lots of snow already that year, so the campus would be gorgeous. There would be a snow sculpture competition, several campus-wide concerts, and a lot of drinking. How could he say no?

The pair left late Friday and arrived at Bates right before the bar scene started, meeting Jeff's friend Lewis. The three first got trashed. Jeff and Doron then crashed on the floor in the common area of Lewis's dorm. On Saturday, they awoke with a start, hearing the melodies and discordances of an a cappella group practicing. Lewis entered the room and introduced a friend of his, Kate, and a friend of hers named Amy, who was up for the weekend from the Boston area. Amy was a high school senior, had applied to Bates, and was eagerly waiting for her acceptance.

The three guys and two girls spent the entire day together, and something clicked between Doron and Amy. It turned out they had a lot in common. They liked Indian food, craft beer, Led Zeppelin, and Guns N' Roses. In addition, they were JINOs ("Jews in name only").

On Sunday, they all went together to the Bates Puddle Jump, where Batesies would jump into a hole cut in the ice of Lake Andrews. They all participated, but Doron and Amy hadn't known to bring bathing attire, so they jumped in together in their underwear, holding hands. A picture was taken, which made it into the next edition of the *Bates Student*.

Doron and Amy exchanged phone numbers, and Doron called Amy when they were back in Boston. The two started dating seriously. They broke up in late summer, just before Amy left for her freshman year at Bates. Doron didn't see the relationship as long-term, and Amy didn't want to tie herself down at college. While they were dating, as I later learned, Amy spent most weekends at Doron's house, telling Rachel and me she was going to visit a camp friend who lived in Wellesley.

When she finally told us she had been seeing a guy she had met at the Bates Winter Carnival, we were rather surprised and asked for details about who he was, where he lived, and how she had found time to see him. Her answers were bare-bones and elusive. She told us his name was Jack, he lived in the Boston area, and he attended community college. "He's a fine young man and professionally motivated," she added. Rachel had made a face when Amy mentioned the community college aspect.

"How old is he?" Rachel asked.

"He just turned…twenty-two."

"What the hell?" said Rachel. "And you're seventeen. I shouldn't need to tell you how inappropriate that is. He could almost be…your *much* older brother. And how did you find time to see him, if I may be so bold as to ask?"

"We would hang out on weekends."

"Without telling us?"

"Well, I sort of told you. I said I was going to Karen's. Sometimes Jack would meet us there. Sometimes I would just head straight to his apartment. I didn't tell you because I didn't want to upset you. I'm almost an adult, you know. I turn eighteen in September."

"I have no words," said Rachel. "I am horrified and speechless."

"You are almost an adult," I added, "and soon will be on your own at college. You are solely responsible for the consequences of your actions."

It was a relief that Amy had said the relationship was over.

CHAPTER TWENTY-FIVE

On a warm weekend day in June 1995, I was sitting in the backyard reading the *Boston Globe*. The stories were typical, about world events, college scandals, and happenings in nearby towns. On page 23, I saw an article entitled "Drug Smugglers Caught in the Act." In part it read as follows:

> The US Coast Guard has confirmed the arrest of two individuals trying to smuggle drugs into New England through Gloucester Harbor. Observing odd behavior, one of its vessels boarded a small charter fishing boat heading toward Gloucester at 3:00 a.m. Those on board said they were carrying a cargo of emergency equipment. They pointed to the container but could not produce a manifest for it. During the investigation, the Coast Guard confiscated a backpack allegedly belonging to one of the individuals and containing three kilos of a white substance believed to be cocaine.

Arrested and taken into federal custody were Griffin Carmichael, 27, of Cambridge, and Doron Finberg, 22, of Lynn. The authorities are continuing their investigation.

I didn't think much about it at the time, but a week later I overheard a phone conversation in which Amy was probing someone for details about the same *Boston Globe* article, which she apparently had not seen. Because of Amy's intensity of interest, something seemed amiss.

"Were you just talking about last week's *Boston Globe* article about the two recent drug arrests at sea? I said.

"Yes," Amy answered.

"Why such a high degree of interest?"

"Oh, no reason, in particular. I just like to keep up on what's going on."

I know my daughter very well. She couldn't care less about current events. Her response was an obvious canard, made up on the spur of the moment.

"Do you know one of the guys who was arrested?"

She just stared at me, and the silence was deafening. Eventually she coughed up the truth. Yes, she knew the guy named Doron.

"How?" I asked.

At first Amy didn't want to tell me, but I persisted. Eventually, following my veiled threat to withhold her sophomore-year tuition, she relayed the details. The man she had been dating was named Doron, not Jack, and he is the person identified in the article. She only heard today from her friend on the phone that he had been arrested. She was sorry she had concealed his real name. But she knew nothing about his drug-related activities, and they had recently broken up.

"Please don't tell Mom," Amy pleaded. "She will go berserk."

"I need to, sweetie. This is too important. And it shows that you're not as adult as you think you are. You will mature, no doubt. But dating someone who turns out to be a drug dealer shows plain bad judgment. I know you don't normally do that, but this is an exceedingly bad exception. Please try to be more careful."

"OK," Amy said.

I told Rachel that night and somehow managed to convince her it would be best if she let it go. Yelling at Amy, or even talking to her about it, was not going to change a thing.

CHAPTER TWENTY-SIX

What had happened should hardly have been surprising. *Fishaholic* had been heading back to Gloucester in the wee hours of Friday morning with its running lights on. It was about seven miles offshore when a Coast Guard vessel on a routine shore patrol spotted it, first on radar and then by sight. Nothing about the movement seemed untoward, but it was highly unusual for a vessel to travel toward shore at that late hour. Not having anything else to do, the Coast Guard coxswain on the vessel decided to investigate.

The coxswain set a course of three hundred fifty degrees, planning to proceed at twelve knots to intercept *Fishaholic* about 2.5 miles offshore, roughly on the same latitude as Gloucester. After ten minutes, Griff thought he heard something in the distance off the port side of the bow. He then saw a light beam approaching, scanning the water in front, and decided this was not good. "Doron," he said. "Put the boat on full throttle and turn a little to starboard. I think we're being followed." Doron did as he was told.

After about a minute, the radar operator on the Coast Guard vessel noticed that *Fishaholic* had changed course and was heading north, perhaps toward New Hampshire waters. That in and of itself was not troubling because the Coast Guard has jurisdiction in all US waters. But it did suggest a possible attempt to evade the law, so he told the coxswain, who immediately ordered a change of course and an increase in speed to twenty knots. The cutter could go up to forty knots, if necessary.

"Not a good sign," said Griff as he saw the boat that had been following them speed up and veer to the right. "I'm not sure what we can do about this."

His immediate thought was to get the backpack and toss it overboard after weighing it down with a piece of anchor chain. But he had to make a quick decision. If he took that approach, the cocaine would be gone for eternity. That would not make his New England partners happy; that was for sure. And he'd still owe money to his Colombian contacts. Perhaps a better solution would be to hide the backpack and talk his way out of this once the approaching vessel arrived. He still didn't know what kind of boat was approaching, but he assumed it was the Coast Guard or Harbor Patrol.

Griff didn't have to wait long to figure it out. As the boat came closer, the strobe light was focused on *Fishaholic*, and a voice blared over a megaphone: "This is the Coast Guard. Heave to and reduce your engine to an idle. You are about to be boarded." Doron did as directed while Griffin hid the backpack in plain sight, with the life jackets and other gear in the forward cabin.

After the Coast Guard cutter pulled up alongside *Fishaholic*, the boarding party of four went aboard. The chief boarding officer demanded to see Doron's maritime license. Doron retrieved it from the left breast pocket of his windbreaker and thrust it toward the officer, who merely glanced at it before beginning his questioning.

"Where are you going so late at night?"

"We're heading into Gloucester Harbor," Doron said.

"Where are you coming from?"

Before Doron could answer, Griffin responded, "Portsmouth, New Hampshire," in an insistent tone.

"And why are you at sea so late at night?"

Griffin continued the narrative he was making up on the fly: "We were visiting friends and had a few beers, which delayed our departure. We need to get back so we can go to work in the morning."

"How many beers did you have? "

"We each had two," Griffin answered.

"Are you drunk?"

"Of course not," said Griffin.

"Then the two of you won't mind taking a breathalyzer test."

"Sure," said Griffin, "that would be fine."

The boarding officer's aide administered the test, which showed a blood alcohol level of 0.04 for each of them.

"How much do you weigh, Mr. Finberg?"

"One hundred sixty pounds."

"You?" the boarding officer asked, pointing at Griff.

"One hundred eighty."

"That means you're both on the cusp," the aide said. "Mr. Finberg, you're lucky. You're not legally intoxicated, so I'm not going to issue a citation. But I'm warning you that your reading shows you are somewhat impaired. In the future, stay away from drinking before operating a vessel."

It appeared that the Coast Guardsmen were going to leave Griffin and Doron alone, and each gave a quiet sigh of relief. But the boarding officer immediately pointed at the trunk in the middle of the cockpit and said, "What's in there?"

Doron and Griffin glanced at each other for a millisecond before Griffin again took the lead, saying, "Oh, just some emergency medical equipment we went to Portsmouth to retrieve. We're planning to bring it to the Gloucester Volunteer Fire and Rescue station. They were running low on supplies."

"Mind if we have a look?" the boarding officer asked.

"Go ahead," said Griffin, as he opened the lid.

Inside was the emergency equipment that Doron had fortunately remembered to bring on board before they left the dock in Gloucester.

The boarding officer was silent and began to scratch his head. "There are a couple of things that don't make sense to me," he said. "First, there's the inconsistency in your story. A few minutes ago, you said you were in Portsmouth visiting friends and had a few beers with them. Now you say you are transporting emergency equipment from Portsmouth to Gloucester. Which is it?"

"It's both, actually," said Doron. "We needed to go to Portsmouth to pick up the equipment, and we took the opportunity to visit friends."

"Maybe," said the boarding officer. "But it only takes an hour or so to drive from Portsmouth to Gloucester, and it takes much longer to go by boat. It's curious you would take a boat. And one other thing. We tracked you on a due-west compass course to shore. If you were coming from Portsmouth, you would have a southwest heading, say about 210 degrees. I think you're hiding something, so we're going to search your boat.

"You can't do that," said Griffin. "You need a warrant, and you don't have one."

"You think you're a real smartass," the boarding officer said. "You must have watched a lot of *Law & Order* shows on TV. If you knew the law, you'd be aware that 18 U.S.C. 89 (a) gives the Coast Guard sweeping authority to board, inspect, and search boats like yours in US waters. Sorry, bud—I think we need to do a complete vessel inspection."

The boarding officer drew his gun, training it on Griffin, and called for two more Coast Guardsmen to board the *Fishaholic*. They did and helped the aide conduct the search. After donning plastic gloves, the three of them lifted the cockpit cushions and examined the storage wells underneath. They went into the cabin and looked under the cushions. The examined the head and galley carefully. Then they entered the forward cabin, which held several life jackets, the anchor, and some fishing gear. There, thrown on top of the gear, they found Griffin's backpack.

The Coast Guardsman held it up for others to see and declared, "Ah, now this is interesting." He carefully unzipped it and peered inside, expecting to see a weapon. But he did not. Instead, he saw three manmade bricks of a white substance encased in clear plastic. He immediately notified the boarding officer, who declared to Doron and Griffin, "We are seizing this vessel and putting you under arrest." Another Coast Guardsmen handcuffed Doron and Griffin.

Things moved quickly after that. Doron and Griffin were escorted onto the Coast Guard vessel, and *Fishaholic* was towed to Gloucester, where it was formally impounded. The white bricks were sent to the federal crime lab, where they were tested for fingerprints. Less than a day later, the test results came back. The bricks were cocaine, and Griffin's fingerprints were on them. Griffin and Doron were arraigned the following day in federal court in Boston. Each was charged with multiple counts of possession, drug trafficking, and conspiracy.

CHAPTER TWENTY-SEVEN

Early in the morning after they were processed, Griffin and Doron made their allowed telephone calls. Griffin called Bull & Bird, a small firm in Boston specializing in criminal defense work. It was the same firm used by the cartel from time to time when legal problems arose. Griffin carried the card of Bob Poindexter, the head litigator, in his wallet.

Doron didn't have a clue whom to call, so he called his father. When he told Artem he was in jail and needed help, Artem's first reaction was to raise his voice, shouting, "What do you mean you're in jail? That can't be. This is going to ruin my reputation."

After Artem calmed down a bit, he asked Doron what he had done. "Nothing, Pop," said Doron. He explained that the Coast Guard had found cocaine on *Fishaholic*, in Griffin's backpack. Doron added that he knew nothing about it and was totally innocent. But he needed a lawyer. Could his father help find him one?

Artem knew better than to think Doron's supposed lack of knowledge would get him off the hook. Perhaps the government could prove that Doron should have known about the cocaine. Also, Artem's boat had been impounded, and he wanted it back. Artem was angry at himself for allowing himself to be hoodwinked. He didn't need the extra money that the nighttime charter generated, but he had gone along with the plan to build up the size of his estate for his children and to show Ricky that he trusted him. Artem told Doron to sit tight while he found a lawyer. He knew several from the synagogue, but only one, Randy Tepper, practiced criminal law. He was a named partner at Tepper and Tepper. Artem called him and asked if he would represent Doron. Tepper immediately agreed to the request and headed to the processing center to visit Doron. Artem advanced a sizable retainer and paid the $100,000 necessary for Doron's release on a $1 million bond.

The local press was all over the story. Initially there were multiple pieces published about the arrest and indictment, including the one I had seen in the *Boston Globe*. The media followed the case tenaciously, interviewing the assistant US attorney in charge from time to time, trying to garner the facts. It became clear that the activities alleged in the indictment related to an ongoing federal investigation into New England drug importation and distribution.

Although Doron was out on bail, it took almost a year for the case to go to trial. At the eleventh hour, Doron accepted a deal under which he would plead guilty to one count of drug possession, pay a $10,000 fine, and testify for the government in any related prosecutions. In return, the government would recommend that the judge impose a three-year suspended sentence and two hundred hours of mandatory community service. Attorney Tepper said that this was the best deal Doron could expect, so Doron grabbed it.

Griffin was not let off as easily. He refused to tell the prosecutors where he had obtained the cocaine, although they had a fairly good idea. If he told them, Griffin knew that his head would be on the line, quite literally, as the cartel did not respond kindly to snitches. He also didn't see any point in flipping on his New England business partners because there would be nothing to gain unless he also revealed details about the cartel. His attorney requested his release on bail pending trial, but the prosecutor argued he was a flight risk, which he probably was, and the judge denied bail. Griffin thus accepted his fate: he would rot in jail until after the conclusion of the trial, at the earliest. He knew that his trial might be delayed until the completion of the ongoing investigation about the New England drug trade.

Artem asked Randy Tepper to represent him in an effort to retrieve *Fishaholic*, but those efforts were in vain. The government argued that the boat was needed as evidence in an ongoing criminal investigation and in any event was subject to forfeiture because it had been used in the crime for which his son had just pled guilty. Getting the boat back is a long shot, Tepper had told Artem.

Early on when these events were unfolding, Artem had called his son Ricky to see if he knew anything about the drug trafficking operation that the government was investigating. Ricky said no, although he, of course, had some inkling. Although not religious, Ricky prayed to whatever god would listen to protect his own involvement from seeing the light of day.

CHAPTER TWENTY-EIGHT

On September 28, 1995, almost fifteen years to the day after Maia Murphy went missing, three twelve-year-old boys were playing in Ravenswood Park in Gloucester. The historic site of Gloucester's first settlers in 1623, the park had a beautiful, secluded beach but also lots of hiking trails through the adjoining woods. The boys were at the gazebo and decided to play a game of hide-and-seek. One, Bradley, volunteered to look for the other two. "I'll count to a hundred," he said, "while you go and hide. I bet there are a lot of places near here, along the water or in the woods. The only place out of bounds is the water itself. I don't intend to get soaked going after you."

Both other boys immediately ran to the woods, where they split up and headed in different directions. Joey soon found an old oak tree with thickets of hollies around it. He pushed his way into the hollies and saw a large pile of leaves that must have been formed naturally by the winds that regularly swept the park.

Jude decided to head deeper into the park in search of a good hiding place and maybe some adventure. He hightailed it along one of the trails and saw what looked like it could have been a narrow Pawtucket Indian trail weaving up a steep hill into the woods. Somewhere up there he might find the perfect hiding place, so he set out along the trail. He needed to be careful. The trail was steep and strewn with exposed tree roots and rocks. With one misstep, Jude might have fallen and broken his ankle. Or he could have slid backward down the trail and over the cliff into more woods fifty feet below.

The going was tough, even for an agile twelve-year-old. Eventually, Jude reached a small clearing, which appeared to contain the extinguished ashes of a campfire. He looked for a safe haven near there in the woods. He found what he thought was one, headed for it, and crouched down, sliding one hand into the leaves below. He touched something that he thought must be a stick. When he pulled it out, he shrieked and then shouted, "Yuck, this looks like a bone." Maybe it was from a deer, he thought. Then he looked to his left. About five feet away, half buried in the dirt, he saw a protrusion that looked like a skull. Could that be from a human? he asked himself. It certainly was no deer.

The game of hide-and-seek was suddenly over. Jude yelled to Bradley and Joey, "Come quickly. I might have found something terrible."

The two boys ran as fast as they could, with Joey arriving first. "Oh God in heaven," Joey said. "That looks like a dead body." Bradley arrived a few moments later and confirmed the diagnosis.

"Someone needs to stay here," Bradley said. "Why don't I do it, while the two of you go to get help?"

Joey and Jude agreed to the plan. They ran as fast as they could through the park to the ranger station. Out of breath, they simultaneously shouted "Help!" to the first person they saw in uniform. After breathing normally again and gaining his composure, Joey explained that Jude had found what they all thought were old bones from a human body.

Several rangers went back to the site with Joey and Jude. They, too, thought it was a human body. "Don't touch anything," one of the rangers said to the boys. They radioed back to the ranger station and told the receptionist to summon the police and the coroner as quickly as possible.

Three police cruisers arrived at Ravenswood Park fifteen minutes later with their sirens blaring, with a total of six officers. They were followed immediately by a K9 vehicle with an officer and two dogs. Five minutes after that, the coroner and his forensic team arrived. One of the rangers escorted them all to what now appeared to be a crime site. Officer Sheffield told the boys to stand back. He immediately saw the bone and partially exposed skull, noting on the clipboard that only one of the boys had touched the bone. The police put yellow tape around the perimeter and started their search.

First, an officer photographed the area after placing a number one marker by the skull and a number two marker by the bone. Then, the team progressed to the evidence-collection phase. An officer started with the skull, gently removing dirt from around it and placing it in a plastic evidence bag. Then he moved to the bone. "It looks like a human femur," he said. After placing it in another evidence bag, he began to remove nearby leaves, one by one. After the area was cleared, he saw what looked like a slight indentation and began to remove dirt with a hoe. Another bone appeared, followed by yet another. That was enough for the police to start excavating the whole area. They found more bones in the ever-expanding hole, some jutting from clothing that could have belonged to Maia. With the help of the dogs, they also found a white Nike sneaker, half eaten by worms, about five yards away in the underbrush. It had a red heart-shaped charm tied in the laces. Much farther away, they found another remote clearing that appeared to have been a campfire site at one time or another. Next to that clearing, in more underbrush, they found some old cigarette butts, three beer bottles, and a conch shell.

One of the officers immediately remembered that a girl had disappeared from Gloucester about ten years earlier and was never found. He uttered this out loud and said to no one in particular, "I wonder if these could be her remains."

"Hard to know," said a second officer. "Forensics will have a field day with this new evidence."

Another officer chimed in. "I think her name was Maia Murphy," he said. "They found her backpack near the gazebo, along with her bike, but not much else. If these are her remains, I wonder what happened to her clothes."

Two weeks after the team had departed from Ravenswood Park with evidence bags in hand for further analysis, the coroner issued his report. In it, he concluded that the remains were in fact those of Maia Murphy. DNA found in tissue extracted from one of the bones was a 99 percent match to DNA extracted from hair in the brush in Maia's backpack, found in the park at the time of her disappearance. The police had held on to this evidence for all these years, and now, fortunately, it could be put to proper use. The sneaker also appeared to be Maia's. It was a girl's size 6, and Maia's mother would identify it as being hers.

When the police arrived at Maia's house and rang the doorbell, Maia's mother, Carol Murphy, came to the door.

"Yes, how may I help you?" Maia's mother said.

Officer Stabler stared at her, noting that she looked gaunter than when she had appeared at the first police press conference almost a full decade prior. "Ma'am, I'm sorry to have to tell you this," Officer Stabler said, "but we have found your daughter's remains. At some point in the future, we will be able to return them to you for a proper burial."

Maia's mother thrust her face into her hands and began to wail. She kept sobbing for a good three minutes; then she finally calmed down a bit and spat out a series of questions. "What did you find, and where did you find it? How do you know it's Maia? Are you sure? Could it be a mistake?"

The officer explained how and where they had found the body. He told her how they had used DNA testing to confirm the identity. And he showed her a photograph of the sneaker that contained a red heart charm tied to one of the laces. Maia's mom identified the sneaker as Maia's. Reality then hit her like a brick. She finally had to accept the fact that Maia was dead.

She immediately called her husband at work and told him the news. He, too, was devastated. Until then, they had held on to a dim flicker of hope that she would return to them someday. It was a yearning more than a rational thought, but it had persisted for all those years.

That is not to say that the Murphys had not been pragmatic. Shortly after the one-year anniversary of Maia's disappearance, Maia's parents had applied to the court to have her declared legally dead. It was a difficult thing to do, but they had decided that would be the only way to move on.

After obtaining the court order, Maia's parents had planned a funeral. A memorial mass was held at their parish church, and it was bursting at the seams with people who wanted to pay their respects. Most of Maia's classmates attended, as did Rachel and some of the other schoolteachers. Rachel told me how sad the service was. Even the eulogies couldn't do justice to just how remarkable a person Maia had been. Her life had been tragically cut short, and what positive things could you say about that? A lunch reception was held in the church basement immediately after the service. In addition to offering sandwiches and comfort foods, Maia's parents arranged a dessert table with many of Maia's favorite cakes. "Maia would have wanted her friends to celebrate her life, not mourn her death," Carol told her friends.

The discovery of Maia's remains created a new quandary for Kieran and Carol—what to do so many years after the disappearance. Maia had already had a funeral, so they asked themselves whether it made any sense to have another service now. They decided the best course would be to have her remains cremated and then interred in a mausoleum at the church. That was what they did once the new police investigation had been conducted.

Maia's parents asked the police whether the discovery of her remains helped at all in pursuing Maia's killer or killers.

The police said theoretically yes, because they now had a body, but that the problem was finding any new evidence connecting the murder to any one person. The bones and everything else found at the crime scene bore no fingerprints or other biological markers. The police agreed to reopen the case and go through all the evidence again, but they were not optimistic about finding anything helpful.

First, they assigned a new team of detectives to look at the evidence. The team retrieved the evidence box from storage. It contained all the physical evidence—Maia's backpack and its contents, the results of the fingerprint tests on that evidence and Maia's bicycle (which had been returned to Maia's family), Maia's diary, and all the interview reports. It also contained all the other reports, interview notes, and tape recordings.

Then, they appointed each team member to review a designated portion of the record and to share his or her findings with the others. Nothing jumped out to any of the team members as being noteworthy. The evidence still pointed to Mark as being the most likely suspect, but it was weak.

The team also examined the new pieces of evidence, which consisted of the skeleton, the clothing remnants, the sneaker, and the conch shell. The coroner had found no fingerprints on any of those items. He had, however, noticed a slight indentation on the back of Maia's skull. This could be evidence of blunt force trauma to the skull, and the conch shell could have been the cause of that trauma. But it was impossible to make a conclusive determination.

The team spent some time discussing whether the murder was likely to have taken place at the crime site or to have occurred elsewhere; if elsewhere, how and why the body had been moved to the site at which it was found; and why there were only clothing remnants (the clothing had probably decomposed over time). None of these questions were answerable.

In the years since Maia's disappearance, science had advanced substantially, and extraction of DNA from crime scene items had become customary in many jurisdictions throughout the country. Additionally, courts were beginning to accept DNA results to identify criminal perpetrators. Both were true in Essex County, Massachusetts, in which Gloucester is located. The police, therefore, sent all the physical evidence in Maia's case, including the human remains and related items found at the crime scene, to a forensics lab for DNA analysis. Following a painstaking examination, in which it compared DNA in the bones to hair in the hairbrush in Maia's backpack, the testing lab was able to identify the human remains as Maia's. The lab also identified DNA on the conch shell as coming from two different people, Maia and an unknown individual.

At the end of their new examination, the police concluded they had positively identified Maia's remains, but they otherwise were not much further along than previously. They could not definitively identify the cause of death or the unknown person who might have played a part in it. They gathered up all the evidence, including the conch shell, clothing remnants, and sneaker, placed it in the evidence box, and returned it to storage. Everyone thought it would stay there forever, or at least until its disposal sometime in the future.

Kieran and Carol Murphy were disheartened but had re-signed themselves long ago to the prospect that Maia's killer or killers would never be identified.

CHAPTER TWENTY-NINE

It had been almost two years since Doron's arrest and *Fishaholic*'s seizure. Artem had unsuccessfully tried various legal means to get the vessel back. The fact that it had been used in drug smuggling made the task extremely difficult, as the presumption in such cases runs against the vessel owner and in favor of the government. Artem's attorney, Randy Tepper, filed a motion to vacate the seizure order, but the judge shot that down because Artem's own son had been involved in the smuggling event. He was unable to prove that he was an innocent bystander. He was lucky he hadn't himself been charged in a criminal capacity. If the judge had asked to see the charter contract, he might have noticed that Artem Finberg and Griffin Carmichael were both signatories. Had the judge noticed that and realized that Griffin was separately involved in the drug-smuggling incident, he easily could have recommended that the government indict Artem on criminal grounds.

Randy Tepper also challenged the seizure on procedural grounds, arguing that the notice of seizure was legally inadequate. The judge rejected that argument too.

Artem went home and groused to Sylvia that he had to give up on recovering the boat. Sylvia called Ricky to tell him what had happened and that his father was upset. He was considering an appeal on substantive and procedural grounds. Could Ricky think of anything else that might be done to help his father? Ricky said he would think about it and talk to Dad.

In truth, Ricky was aghast because he didn't want his father to do anything that might stir up the hornets' nest and point to broader wrongdoing. He visited his dad the next evening, when Emmy was at a Junior League meeting, and broached the subject. Their son, Hunter, was three years old and at home with the nanny.

"Dad, I'm so sorry you lost the boat, but maybe it's for the best," Ricky said.

"How can you say that? What's good about it?"

"Well, Doron took a plea deal," Ricky said, "and he is required to assist the government in related matters, including testifying in court, if requested to do so. A continuing fight to get the boat back might prompt the government to look further into all the circumstances."

"That seems ridiculous to me," Artem said.

What Ricky didn't tell Artem was that Ricky was concerned about protecting his own skin. He, of course, had a side deal with Griffin, who was still under investigation and indictment. God forbid the nature of that arrangement became public. It would show Ricky's linkage to the drug-smuggling arrangement and probably lead to his own arrest. He had been continually in knots, wondering if today would be the day that he was arrested. He didn't want his father to make things worse, but he also couldn't tell him the true reason. What would he say—that he had been getting a kickback from Griffin and knew from the start that the arrangement into which his father had entered, at his urging, failed to pass the smell test?

In the end, Artem said OK, that he wouldn't pursue the matter any further. "This is just another example of something you have screwed up."

Meanwhile, the government had completed its broader drug-trafficking investigation and concluded that the incident on *Fishaholic* was part of the Colombian drug smuggling operation. Doron had cooperated, as required by his plea deal, and told the government about his late-night weekly trips to a larger vessel with Griffin on board. He said Griffin had always carried the same backpack out to the larger vessel and then back to Gloucester. He didn't know the name of the larger vessel, and he didn't know what had been brought in the backpack in either direction. But he knew now that the backpack had contained cocaine (because it had been confiscated), and he surmised that it had contained similar drugs on the other trips he had taken. He couldn't say what had been in the backpack on the outbound leg but presumed it was cash.

The government asked Doron what he had been paid for his services. He said, of course, that he had received overtime for the nighttime work and that he'd assumed that came, in part, from the added revenue inuring to Gloucester Sea Charter Outfitters. The government also asked Doron if he'd been paid extra by Griffin. That came as close to disaster as he could have imagined. He truthfully answered no, because the $3,000-per-week payments he had received had been paid to him by Ricky.

Doron didn't want to implicate his brother if there was any way to avoid it, but he knew he had to answer the questions truthfully. If they had asked Doron if he had received compensation from any source other than Gloucester Sea Charter Outfitters, he might have had to say yes. It would have been an agonizing choice between lying and turning on Ricky.

Griffin was summoned from jail on several occasions for questioning by the government. Each time, his lawyer was present, and each time he invoked his constitutional right against self-incrimination. So the government got nothing from him.

Of course, Griffin was worried that if he said anything, the Medellín cartel would put a hit on him. Whether or not it did is subject to conjecture, but on April 7, 1997, Griffin was walking to dinner in a line of prisoners when he suddenly felt a sharp twinge in his back. He looked down and saw blood welling from his abdomen and a long blade protruding from it. Before everything went dark, his last words were "So much for protection of the law."

Ricky worried about his impending arrest for a full five years from the day the *Fishaholic* was seized and the drug-trafficking arrests were made. That was because there was a five-year statute of limitations on drug-trafficking charges. Once five years elapsed, he would be home free. During the months leading to the five-year date, he kept day-to-day track of how many days he had left. He never told a soul about his worries, but that didn't make them any less agonizing. "Perhaps that is my penance," he muttered one day when he was alone. "I have already been punished quite a lot for my bad decision."

A day after the statute of limitations expired, Ricky breathed a huge sigh of relief. He called Doron, who had completed his suspended sentence months before, to see if Doron was free to grab a few beers. Doron said sure, and the two met later at a local bar.

"You look jovial," said Doron.

"It's more that I'm relieved," Ricky said. "I had a big project at work that I just finished. My boss liked the result." Ricky didn't want to mention anything about the statute of limitations. It would just rub in Doron's face that Doron had pleaded guilty for a crime that Ricky had been instrumental in orchestrating.

A week later, Ricky went to his lawyer's office and asked him to draw up divorce papers. He had tried hard to make his marriage work, Ricky told his lawyer, and the two of them just weren't a good fit. He was sure that Emmy would agree to joint custody of Hunter. Emmy and Ricky had a prenuptial agreement, so Ricky knew he wouldn't get any of the Weld assets, but he didn't care. He'd still have his work income and could buy a condo somewhere. He just wanted out of the marriage.

CHAPTER THIRTY

Wednesday, February 20, 2002, was a typical winter day in the Boston area. Snow had fallen on and off over the past few days and turned into a sheet of ice after the nighttime temperature dropped into the single digits. Although the air was crisp, few except hardy souls wanted to go outside.

Rachel picked up the *Boston Globe* and flipped through its pages. On the obituary page, she first noticed an announcement of the death of William Davis Taylor, who had been the newspaper's publisher for many years before retiring in 1977. He had died the previous day at the age of ninety-three. Scion of a well-known Boston family, he had attended the Noble and Greenough School and Harvard University.

Then her eyes darted to another obituary about Artem Finberg of Gloucester. Although she hadn't known Artem well, she immediately recognized his name. According to the article, he had died two days earlier of a stroke at his place of business, Gloucester Sea Charter Outfitters. He had been a pillar of the Gloucester business community, it said, and had won many awards from the local Rotary Club. Over the years, he had raised more than $500,000 for the Rotary Club and a similar amount for his local synagogue. The burial would be held the next day and would be private, with a memorial service to be held at a later date.

Rachel picked up the phone and called me at work. After I answered, she told me what she had read and asked me how well I'd known him. Not well at all, I said, but I reminded her that Amy had dated his son, Doron, briefly some years prior. She had completely forgotten about that.

We both agreed that it wouldn't be necessary for us to go to the memorial service. It would be a nice thing to send his widow, Sylvia, a condolence note, Rachel offered. I agreed, and Rachel said she would take care of it.

I thought it was a shame that Artem had died in his early seventies. When my parents had died in their sixties, I'd thought seventy-two was a ripe old age, but not anymore. My own life was flying by, and before I knew it, I would get there myself (God willing).

CHAPTER THIRTY-ONE

About a year went by before I gave another thought to the Finberg family. It was evening, and I was home from work, flipping through the newspaper like I always did. While Rachel was a close follower of the obituaries, I was drawn to the public notices. You could always find things of interest there—real estate foreclosure notices, exotic cars for sale, and auctions of all sorts of high-end goods that had been confiscated by the government because of their connection to illegal activities. In fact, several months before, I had seen a listing for the auctioning of a fishing trawler, *Fishaholic*, which had been confiscated during a drug raid several years earlier.

On this one occasion, I was jolted to attention by the notice of a planned auction of a business referred to as Gloucester Sea Charter Outfitters. It was listed as a going concern, with assets valued at $5.3 million and liabilities of $8.7 million. Assets consisted mostly of ten charter fishing vessels and $100,000 in cash. The debt consisted mostly of mortgages on the fishing vessels. Because the debt was long term, the size of it might not be problematic to a buyer. On the other hand, I doubted the sellers would get much for the business.

I was intrigued because the Finberg family had a reputation for running a successful business. It frankly shocked me that the finances appeared to be so marginal. After Artem had died, I'd assumed his three sons would take over and continue the business. I realized that something must have gone amiss.

On the following day, I walked into the office of Bob Kurtz, one of my law partners, who also practiced maritime law and kept track of related financial transactions. "Have you seen this?" I asked, pointing to the paper.

"Yes," he said. "My sources told me that the Finberg sons have been running the business to the ground. The eldest and youngest sons have had day-to-day control of the business and haven't kept their eyes on the bottom line. The middle son, Richard, is a whiz, but he's too busy at his own daytime job to devote much attention to the business."

Bob continued, "It's a shame for the widow, who never was involved in the business and trusted her sons. She owns 100 percent of the shares (it's a privately held company) but isn't expected to get much out of the sale. She'll probably net $100,000, which won't sustain her lifestyle. Fortunately, I heard that she came into some money when her parents died."

The auction was scheduled for the following week, and I made it a point to see what happened. It turned out that Bob was right. There were two bidders, but neither was willing to offer too much. The bidding started at $100,000. The successful bidder paid $195,000, out of which a 20 percent commission was taken, leaving Sylvia with $156,000.

The sale of the business meant that Mark and Doron both needed to get jobs, something neither was accustomed to doing. Mark found one at the Cape Ann Transportation Authority, which operated the local transit system. Doron was unemployed for quite a while.

This time was a particularly trying one for Doron. Not the smartest person in the world, or even the Boston area, he didn't have a clue how to find a job. After college, he had gone right to work for his dad and kept at it up through the sale of the business. Even when he was going through his legal problems (to put things mildly), he continued to work in the business when he could, and when he couldn't, he continued to draw a salary. He was getting advice from all corners. Sylvia suggested he move to New York and get a job in the garment business, but that was a dying field. Ricky said he should go back to school and get a useful degree, perhaps as a medical assistant, lab technician, or a library scientist (that's what they used to call a librarian). Not one of those ideas appealed to Doron. Typically, he would hang out at one of the local bars in the evening, and there he would be exposed to other opportunities, if you catch my drift. Someone there told him about opportunities to drive trucks, and he didn't even need to get a professional driver's license. It turned out these were to transport contraband back and forth between Boston and Chicago. Not only was Doron unenthused by the prospect of long nighttime drives, but he also thought it might be a good idea to avoid illegal activities in view of his prior conviction.

One evening, a man who looked vaguely familiar entered the bar he was frequenting at the time. The man looked at Doron, and Doron looked back. A smile emerged from the man's otherwise austere face, and Doron, for his part, showed the first signs of recognition.

The man was Griffin Carmichael. When Doron realized this, his jaw dropped, and he just stared. Griffin stared back, but not in a menacing way, and finally thrust out his hand toward Doron, who took it and shook it.

"Well, I'll be damned," said Griffin. "I never thought I'd come across you in a place like this."

"What the hell?" said Doron. "I thought you were dead. I heard that you had been stabbed to death in prison."

"Stabbed, but not to death," Griffin said.

"So what happened?"

"Well, I was on the line for food, and a guy came up from behind. I didn't see him but felt something thrust through my back. I immediately saw blood oozing out of my stomach and the tip of the knife sticking out in front. I blacked out. The next thing I remember is waking up in Mass General in a private room, shackled to the bed. There were two armed guards in front of my door. I asked a nurse how I got there. She told me I was lucky. I almost died. Had the stab wound been just a little higher, it would have pierced my heart, and that surely would have been the end. But God provides, I guess. The doctors were able to operate. Successfully. I'm now fit as a fiddle."

"But how did you get out of prison? You didn't escape, did you?"

"Ha," Griffin said. "That might have been a good idea. But my story is not nearly as dramatic. I'm sure my stabbing was ordered by the Medellín cartel to keep me from talking about their operation. The feds knew that too. They weren't going to put me back in the same penitentiary. They moved me to the federal maximum-security facility in Florence, Colorado, and there I waited. Eventually, after talking to the prosecutors several times and sharing my limited knowledge about the drug-trafficking operation, they offered me a plea deal, which I took. I had to rat out my partners in our Boston distribution facility, but them's the breaks. I took an eight-year sentence, which was reduced to five years for good behavior. I got out a few months ago."

"What about the cartel?"

The feds didn't have much of anything on the cartel and wouldn't have been able to arrest anyone in Colombia. I think they decided to drop the broader investigation and focus on me and the other guys they caught locally."

"Are you scared about your safety?" Doron asked.

"Not really," said Griffin. "They tried to kill me once and failed. They have informants in the prosecutor's office and must know that the feds have dropped their investigation of the cartel for now. There's no reason for them to go after me again. Needless to say, I'm not working with them anymore."

"What are you doing now?"

"You know. A little bit of this. A little bit of that. Enough to eke out a living. Griffin Entertainment is still operating and doing well. One of our latest ventures is a modeling service. We provide nude models in plush settings to artists who want to paint them and photographers who want to take their pictures. They are tasty ladies, as you might imagine. The hourly fee is high, but the models are worth it, and the demand for our services is strong. You'd be surprised how many amateur painters and photographers we now count among our clientele. Some are judges and high-ranking government officials. Others run some of the top high-tech companies in the Boston area."

"You heard about Emily and Ricky splitting up, I assume," said Doron.

"Yes, that was a real shame," said Griffin. "I think the stress of the nighttime charter operation he helped put together was just too much. How's he doing?"

"He's OK, I guess," Doron said. "I don't see him much. In fact, I don't see my family much at all. We were never close. My dad died last year, and we came together briefly to help my mom. I see her occasionally, but we don't have a close relationship."

"Sorry to hear about your dad. Say, if you ever need a job, I could hire you to work for Griffin Entertainment in one of our modeling studios."

"Thanks, but I'm fine," Doron said. He sometimes was obtuse but knew enough not to dip his pen in Griffin's inkwell a second time.

After three months of frequenting bars and living off the money he had earned doing nighttime charters, Doron found a job as a metals detailer in a local welding company.

CHAPTER THIRTY-TWO

Let's fast-forward to July 23, 2006, a beautiful, sunny day at the US Merchant Marine Academy in Kings Point, New York. Located directly on Long Island Sound and overlooking the Throgs Neck Bridge, the Merchant Marine Academy resembled more of a mansion belonging to one of Jay Gatsby's neighbors in West Egg than a government facility located in its true Kings Point counterpart.

The guests could see the New York City skyline in the distance. In the near waters stood Execution Rocks Lighthouse, erected in 1849 on a pile of rocks between Long Island and Westchester County, NY. The name "Execution Rocks" came from a 1700s practice of the British to execute colonial prisoners by chaining them to the rock pile at low tide and waiting for high tide to roll in before removing the bodies.

The day was significant because it was the fiftieth-anniversary reunion of survivors of the *Andrea Doria* shipwreck and their families. Sylvia Finberg had received an invitation addressed to Artem. Her first thought was to decline the invitation. But after she talked it over with her son Mark, the two of them decided to attend together. Mark, of course, loved boats and was dying to see the fleet of small sailboats on which the midshipmen practiced. Sylvia had heard about the harrowing sinking from Artem. She wanted to talk to some of the other people who had experienced it. She also felt a primordial pull to the representation of the event that had provided the impetus for Artem to establish their New England lifestyle.

When Mark turned off Steamboat Road and drove up to the academy in Sylvia's brand-new ruby-red Lexus SC convertible, the two guards in their dress white uniforms jumped to open both doors simultaneously. They asked if the pair was there to attend the *Andrea Doria* reunion and, hearing an affirmative response, pointed the way to the outdoor patio, where they were to pick up their badges before heading to the cocktail reception. "That's a beautiful automobile," one of the attendants said. "Mind if I ask you the meaning of the license plate?" The plate read "TROLLN."

"Oh, that," Sylvia said. "Until a few years ago, when my husband died, our family had a charter fishing business. We did a lot of trolling for fish."

"Don't you mean *trawling*?"

"Actually, no. Trawling is when you throw a net out over the stern to catch as many fish as possible at one time. Trolling is when you throw out a line with bait attached and motor through the water trying to catch something specific. That's what our customers usually wanted to do—hook and reel in something specific, like a large tuna."

"Ah," the attendant said. "Very clever. I hope you hook and reel in what you're looking for at today's party."

What Sylvia wanted most was to capture a glimpse of Ruth Roman, the famous actress who, she knew, had lost her earrings. Nor would she mind hobnobbing with some of the ship's illustrious passengers, although she was aware that many were much older and probably would be dead by now. Unfortunately, Ruth Roman was not in attendance. Sylvia was unaware that the actress had died seven years earlier.

However, Sylvia found an even better catch at the party. In the corner, in a red dress and white cuff-length calfskin gloves, she spied a woman about her age. She looks familiar, Sylvia thought. Never shy about reaching out to new people, she walked over to the woman and said, "Don't I know you from somewhere?"

"Well, my name is Helen. I live in Prospect Park in Brooklyn. Do we live in the same neighborhood?"

"No, I live in Gloucester, Massachusetts," Sylvia said. "But I grew up in Brooklyn Heights. My parents lived there for many years. My mother recently passed away. My father died years ago, and I'm now trying to decide what to do with the apartment."

"Is it rent controlled?" Helen asked.

"No, it's a co-op owned by my mother's estate. My parents bought it a long time ago when it was converted from a rental building."

"Hmm," Helen said. "You didn't attend Brooklyn College, did you?"

"That's it," Sylvia said. "I graduated in 1955, with a degree in English literature. You?"

"I graduated in 1956 after majoring in business. My parents sent me to Europe for a month after graduation, with my aunt as a chaperone. We were returning in late July 1956 aboard *Andrea Doria* when it sank. Fortunately, we both were rescued and survived. However, it was truly a harrowing experience. That I made it through life until today, fifty years later, is a truly remarkable phenomenon."

"Yes, I can only imagine," said Sylvia. "I am here because my late husband was a steward on the ship and on board when it sank. He was one of the lucky ones to make it off safely." She didn't go into any more detail than that.

"What was your last name?" Helen asked Sylvia.

"It was Rothman, Sylvia Rothman. I'm now Sylvia Finberg."

"So your husband's name was Finberg? What was his first name?

"It was Artem," Sylvia said. "For some reason, the ship's management liked guests to call crew members by short nicknames. On the first day of work, they handed him a nametag with 'Art' imprinted on it, and that's what he was called on the ship. After the last voyage, he couldn't wait to get rid of it. He always hated being called Art or Artie."

"Well, I don't remember any stewards by that name. There was a guy named Valentino, inaptly shortened to Val, and he certainly lived up to his name. He kept pouring more champagne into my glass and whispering that I should meet him on the bow at midnight after his shift was over. I was tempted to do that, throwing caution to the wind, but never felt that unencumbered.

"But you do look familiar to me too," Helen added. She thought for another minute, which seemed to Sylvia to be an eternity.

"I remember you now," said Helen. "We were in a theater production together. You played Birdie in *The Little Foxes* when I played Regina."

"Oh my God," said Sylvia. "I remember you too. But I can't think of your last name."

"It was Koppelman. It's now Newman. You might also recall my cousin, Murray Koppelman, who graduated in 1957. He's a well-known businessman now. He gave lots of money to the college, and the business school is now named after him."

"I don't remember him. Were you at the cast party after the last production of *The Little Foxes*? What an insane event."

"Yes, I was there," said Helen, "and I'm not proud of the fact that I shed my top and started to dance around wearing only my necklace. I must have had too much to drink."

This brief encounter set the stage for an ongoing relationship between Helen and Sylvia. They exchanged addresses—Helen's in Prospect Park and Sylvia's in Gloucester.

Something in Sylvia's conversation with Helen must have hit a chord, because on the long drive home, Sylvia poured out her heart to Mark about how hard things had been for her since Artem's death. Normally, she and Mark did not converse in such an intimate fashion. During the car ride, she explained that she liked living in Gloucester but that it had never felt like home to her. While paired with Mark's dad, she'd felt part of a privileged Jewish couple. She was proud to have been able to make things happen at the synagogue and around town. But without him, she felt lost.

Mark responded in kind. Ordinarily, he would have brushed aside Sylvia's comments. Their typical interaction was asking each other "How was your day?" Probably because Mark lacked intellectual prowess, Sylvia was never proud of Mark, as a mother should be of her son, and Mark could always tell. He had never verbalized those feelings. This time, however, Mark felt moved by his mother's candor and told her so. It was as if they were having a true conversation for the very first time.

Mark told Sylvia how he had always felt eclipsed by Ricky, who had been the better student and had a plan for himself in life. The feeling of rejection was subtle but unmistakable, and it had come mostly from his father but sometimes from his mother as well. He'd wanted nothing more in life than to captain vessels for Gloucester Sea Charter Outfitters and had received multiple mixed messages. Artem had appeared grateful for the help but expected his children strive for more.

With a tear dripping from each eye, Mark then told her how devastated he had been when she had decided to sell the company. "You never even asked me if I could continue to run it," he pointed out. "I could have, and it would have become the Finberg legacy. Wouldn't you have liked that?"

"Oh, darling," Sylvia said. "I'm so sorry that you feel that way. If I could have kept the business and let you run it, I would have. It wasn't doing well financially. You must have known that. The debts were above the level of the assets. Our financial adviser told us we had to dump it, and I believe he was right. The money I received from the sale did not make me a wealthy woman. Thank goodness I received a nice inheritance from Grandma Doris. I should be able to live nicely on that. But unfortunately, I'm unable to help you out financially."

"I never asked for your help," Mark responded with a twinge of annoyance in his voice. "I was just explaining my feelings. I know you will do what you want, and that's OK with me."

"Speaking of that, I've been giving a lot of thought to the idea of moving back to Brooklyn, into Grandma Doris's apartment. I've grown a bit tired of Gloucester. The people at the synagogue are nice, but we have different values. They are New Englanders at heart. I miss Brooklyn, with all its dirt, noise, and street odors. I want to be able to walk across the bridge to Katz's Deli to pick up whitefish, bagels, and knishes.

"Talking to Helen today helped me cement my decision. As soon as we get back, I'm going to put the house on the market. With any luck, I'll be on my way by the end of the fall."

"Oh, I see," Mark said. He turned up the radio, and the two drove in silence until they reached Gloucester.

CHAPTER THIRTY-THREE

In 1994, reacting to the improvement in criminal investigations afforded by DNA analysis over the years, Congress had passed a law directing the US Federal Bureau of Investigation to establish a DNA database of criminal offenders to assist federal and state law enforcement authorities in identifying, apprehending, and convicting perpetrators of certain crimes, including violent offenses. The FBI's Combined DNA Index System, or CODIS, became operational in October 1998 and proved to be a great success. Over the years, as DNA analysis became more sophisticated, CODIS enabled the authorities to solve more and more crimes. For recent and future crimes, the impact was virtually instantaneous. Analysis of past crimes took longer because it occurred slowly over time as law enforcement resources permitted.

DNA similarities are measured in centimorgans, or cMs. Geneticists use cM calculations to measure the degree of genetic linkage between individuals. According to the National Human Genome Research Institute, one cM "is a unit of measure for the frequency of genetic recombination. One centimorgan is equal to a 1% chance that two markers on a chromosome will become separated from one another due to a recombination event during meiosis (which occurs during the formation of egg and sperm cells)." Every human being has 6,800 cMs, 3,400 of which are inherited from each biological parent.

In layman's terms, the more cMs two individuals share, the more they are linked genetically and the more probable it is that they are close relatives. Full siblings generally share between 2,200 and 3,400 cMs, or between 37.5 percent and 61 percent of the total cM count of 6,800—or 50 percent of their cMs, on average. First cousins share between 4 percent and 23 percent, or 12.5 percent on average. For identical twins, there is always a 100 percent cM match.

On a frigid day in January 2010, Officer Presser was sitting at his desk in the Gloucester Police Department when the phone rang. It was the coroner's office, calling to tell him there had been a DNA hit on one of his old cases. The Gloucester Police Department had gone back to Maia Murphy's file. They'd found the DNA on the conch shell in the evidence box, which now enabled them to create a full DNA profile. After conducting a DNA comparison through CODIS, they'd found similarities to Doron Finberg's DNA, which had been included in the initial database because of his prior arrest. The cM match was 1 percent, meaning that the perpetrator was probably a distant relative.

In 2010, Doron was still working at the metal-welding company, so he was easy to track down. The police especially wanted to ask him how to locate his older brother Mark, whose DNA might be a better match than Doron's to the DNA found on the conch shell. They hoped to collect and analyze Mark's DNA, because Mark had never been ruled out as a suspect in Maia Murphy's disappearance. They also wanted Doron to assist them in identifying other, more distant relatives who potentially could be closer DNA matches to the perpetrator.

Two police officers drove to Doron's place of employment, entered through the front door, and asked to speak to him. The company receptionist called over the intercom, "Doron Finberg, please come to the office immediately. Two officers of the law are here to question you about certain police matters."

Doron was angry when he heard the announcement. There was no need for the receptionist to have identified who was there, or the purpose of the visit. As he walked from his workstation to the main office, many people glared at him, increasing his rage exponentially.

When he finally arrived at the company office, Doron greeted the officers coolly and waited patiently for them to explain what they wanted. After they did so, Doron reluctantly decided it would be in his interest to cooperate. He gave them Mark's address and telephone number. Then they asked him about his relatives.

Doron knew his biological family was extensive, but he didn't have information about many of its members. In addition to his parents and brothers, he had lots of great-aunts and great-uncles on both his father's and his mother's sides of the family. One great-aunt and great-uncle had had thirteen children, and many of them had married and had children of their own. Several other great-aunts and great-uncles also had families, although not as large. Some extended families made it a point to get together at weddings and other special occasions and even scheduled family reunions at nice resorts. That was not so for the Finbergs or Sylvia's relatives, the Rothmans. Doron told the police all he knew, but the information wasn't helpful.

The police then reached out to Sylvia, who also came in for questioning. She was able to provide some information about various relatives of hers and Artem's, but this was mostly limited to names and last known geographical locations. And many names of relatives' children and grandchildren completely escaped her. Sylvia couldn't help boasting that she had grown up in Brooklyn Heights in a learned and sophisticated family, so the suspect must be on Artem's side of the family.

The police asked Sylvia if she would mind providing a sample of her own DNA. At first, she was hesitant and asked how it would help. They explained that a comparison with the suspect's DNA could narrow the scope of their search. Sylvia was persuaded and allowed the officers to administer a DNA test on the spot. They knew her DNA would not be a close match and they still would have countless hours of research ahead of them before they could create a comprehensive family tree and attempt to figure out where the suspect fit might into it.

The police also reached out to Mark and Ricky for DNA samples. At first both refused, telling the police they were concerned about giving up their privacy rights.

In pitching the idea to Mark, the police explained that if his DNA was not a 100 percent match to the sample, they could rule him out. This would be advantageous, they said, because he had been a person of interest at the time of the initial investigation. Wouldn't it be better to clear his name now, once and for all?

"Nope," he said, "I'm not doing it. If I do, I'll be in the system forever, and I don't want that. Who knows—my DNA might end up being sold to a database in China or Russia."

There was no convincing Mark otherwise.

Ricky, on the other hand, seemed a bit more amenable. It took some persuading, but he finally agreed to provide a DNA sample. A policeman swabbed his inner cheek on the spot.

The results came back a week later. Sylvia shared 5 percent of her DNA with the unknown suspect, meaning that she and the suspect were likely second cousins. Ricky and the suspect shared 2 percent of their DNA. The test results allowed the police to rule out Sylvia and Ricky as possible killers. Because Mark was also Sylvia's and Artem's son, Mark's DNA should be in the same range as Ricky's. There was no longer any need for the police to seek his DNA. He could not have been the killer.

The police could have pursued this line of inquiry further by conducting a familial search on the Finberg family to determine possible suspects among more distant relatives. However, without having other DNA samples to triangulate, the process would have been laborious and unlikely to produce results. Therefore, as most police departments would do in similar circumstances, the Gloucester Police Department decided to abandon its active search. Should new DNA matches crop up in the future, it would reevaluate the situation.

CHAPTER THIRTY-FOUR

In 2015, when I was about to turn sixty-five, I started to think about my life's unfinished business. I still hungered to find information about my biological family. It would be useful medically, as I was at the age when new, unwanted things were starting to happen. Because I knew my biological maternal grandmother had died of colon cancer at thirty-eight years old, I had already started to get colonoscopies. Also, at that time, doctors were increasingly asking about family medical histories, and I didn't have any more information to share.

I also felt a stronger need to learn who I was. There were television shows about people who found their birth mothers, fathers, and siblings. For many of those people, finding their families was like a burst of white light. Suddenly they knew their roots. In many cases, there was a remarkable reunion of one type or another—usually with a mother or sibling. Although I didn't expect that type of dreamy ending, I felt I deserved to learn as much as I could.

About that time, more and more information about DNA websites was sprouting up. By submitting a DNA sample, you would learn about your genetic ethnicity. If you granted consent, the website would also compare your DNA to other samples and let you know if there were any genetic links, in instances where the parties were agreeable.

After mulling the idea over for about a second, I decided to take the plunge. I ordered a DNA kit from AncestryDNA, spat in the test tube, mixed the saliva with the primer, and sent the sample in for testing. Not knowing what to expect was frightening and formidable.

I waited and waited, hoping eventually to get a match of some sort, probably with a distant relative. Perhaps someday I could figure out where I fit into someone's family tree. Quite something else ended up occurring.

I was at home one evening when my cell phone rang. I answered it.

"Is this Mr. Dreyer?" the caller asked.

"Yes, it is. Who is this, please?"

"This is Detective Sean Connor from the Gloucester Police Department. Do you have a few minutes to talk?"

"Sure," I said. "What's this about?"

"You probably will find this strange, but we are in the midst of an ongoing investigation of a cold case. Back in 1980, there was a Gloucester girl who went missing. It was all over the news."

"Wow," I said, "I remember that case. The girl was in my wife's class at the Fuller School."

"That's right," said Detective Connor. "Her name was Maia Murphy. At the time, everyone hoped she would be found alive. But she wasn't. In fact, she was never found at all until 1995, when human remains were found at Ravenswood State Park, which turned out to be hers.

"To cut to the chase," Detective Connor continued, "we have reopened the case and found a DNA sample on what we think was the murder weapon. We compared the suspect's DNA to other DNA samples available to us in various online databases, including CODIS, AncestryDNA, 23andMe, and GEDmatch, and have periodically updated the comparison. Initially we had one match, but that individual and the suspect were only distant relatives. We are still trying to follow up with relatives of that individual, but the process is time consuming."

"I understand what you are saying," I broke in, "but what does that have to do with me?"

"We just had a second match, through AncestryDNA," he said, "and that match is you."

It felt like the wind had been blown out of my sails.

"Are you saying I'm related to the murderer?" I asked.

"Afraid so," Detective Connor answered. "I'm contacting you because we'd like to learn about your own biological ancestry so we can try to complete the picture."

"I'm afraid I can't help you there," I said, "because I was adopted. I don't know much about where I came from, other than what I learned from the New York adoption agency. That's why I signed up on AncestryDNA."

"What can you tell me?"

"Not too much. My mother was an unwed Jewish woman who couldn't take care of a child. Oh, and my birth name was Michael Eisen. I assume that means my mother's last name was Eisen, but I'm not certain."

"Oh, even that information could end up being helpful. The suspect's last name is not Eisen, but perhaps we can figure out some linkage."

"Wait a minute," I barked. "If I am a match to the suspect and another individual also is a match, does that mean that the other individual and I have DNA in common?"

"That's correct, but unfortunately, I can't tell you anything more than that. It would breach confidentiality."

I suppose I understand why you can't tell me the identity of the other individual. Can you at least tell me how closely we are related?

"Nope. Sorry."

"Are you able to tell the other individual that you have found a DNA match between him and me, and give him my contact information if he wants it?"

"What makes you think it's a he and not a she?" Detective Connor asked.

"Oh, you're right. I just assumed. It could easily be a woman."

"Well, I can't tell you whether it is a man or a woman," Detective Connor said.

"Why not?"

"Same reason. Confidentiality."

"Well, what about my request to tell the other man or woman that I exist and would like to get in touch?"

"I can't do that either," Detective Connor said. "I'd be telling that individual that he or she has a relative he never knew existed. He or she might not want that information, and I can't be the one to offer it."

"So you are saying I have to wait patiently and good-naturedly for that person to register on AncestryDNA, if he or she decides to do that. Am I right?

"Yep," he said.

"Wow," I responded.

After we ended the conversation, I told Rachel about it. I quipped that perhaps I should try to break into the police station to find the other DNA report.

"Not a great idea," she deadpanned.

CHAPTER THIRTY-FIVE

A week before Christmas in 2016, the Boston metropolitan area was decked in festive lights, and office Christmas parties were in full swing. One, in particular, was being held by a high-tech firm at Legal Seafood on the Boston waterfront. It would have been hard for the revelers not to have a good time. Mounds of raw oysters and large cooked shrimp were presented on ice. Hot seafood stew, barbequed ribs, and lobster mac and cheese were in abundance. Of course, the waiters and waitresses also were making their rounds frequently with trays of champagne, wine, and stronger alcoholic beverages.

One middle management employee, Scott Miller, was especially relishing his surroundings. He had just finished a large work project, thankfully before Christmas. That meant he'd have time to take off a couple of days from work. Maybe he, his wife, and their two boys could even fit in a long weekend skiing at Waterville Valley in New Hampshire.

As Scott was about to pick up an oyster, his work colleague, Sandy, sauntered up and gave him a big hug. She was in her early thirties, at least a decade younger than he, and she was close to a Marilyn Monroe lookalike. It was obvious she had

had far too much to drink. After she hugged him, she whispered a question: "Would you like to get a hotel room together tonight?"

While flattered by the overture, Scott knew he had to say no. He loved his wife and didn't want to screw up his marriage over a one-night fling. He politely declined the invitation and then told himself he'd better get out of there. He collected his coat and headed down in the elevator to the street, where he handed the valet his parking stub. "Are you sure you're OK to drive, sir?" the valet asked. "We can call you a cab."

"I am absolutely fine," Scott answered.

A few minutes later, his firetruck-red Porsche 911 pulled up in front, and Scott got in. He had had a couple of drinks but was not inebriated, he told himself. And it would take only thirty minutes to get home.

Not far from the restaurant, just before he was about to exit onto Interstate 93 North to head home, he saw blinking lights behind him. "Oh geez," he said. "This is unfortunate." He pulled over, and a policeman got out of his cruiser and walked over. The policeman asked for Scott's license and registration, which Scott readily handed over.

Then, the police officer told Scott to step out of his vehicle. He did and asked what he had done wrong. "Did you not see that traffic light?" the officer asked. "It was red, and you went right through it."

Scott said he hadn't seen the light and apologized profusely. He thought he might get off with a warning, but the officer then said he'd have to give Scott a breathalyzer test. If Scott refused, the officer said, he'd have to bring him in to the station.

Scott took the test, failed it, and was taken into custody. They told him at the police station he'd be held overnight and arraigned in the morning. They allowed him to call his wife, whom he told to call the family's lawyer. He knew the drill. He had had two prior DUIs, although the last one fortunately had been three years earlier.

His lawyer appeared at the police station promptly at 9:00 a.m. the next morning. After the arraignment, Scott was able to post bail and go home.

Scott was charged with a felony DUI because of his two prior convictions. Technically punishable by imprisonment, this charge almost never resulted in a jail sentence. By pleading guilty, Scott would receive only a fine of $1,000 and a six-month suspension of his driver's license. Scott's lawyer told him it was a good deal and he should take it, which he did. That was when Scott's real problems began.

Under chapter 22E, section 3 of the Massachusetts General Laws, "any person who is convicted of an offense that is punishable by imprisonment in the state prison...shall submit a DNA sample to the department or the commissioner of probation." That applied to Scott and meant Scott was going to have his DNA taken.

Scott didn't think anything of it until a police officer approached him during the release process. They had run his DNA through CODIS, and it had come back as an exact match to the suspect in an old murder case. The confidence interval was 99 percent. Scott was under arrest.

The officer brought Scott to a holding cell to await interrogation. He was read his Miranda rights and told the police would like to question him. He agreed, even though he knew he could remain silent and wait for his attorney.

Scott had almost forgotten about that fateful day in 1980 when he had offered a ride on his boat to that girl and things had gone awry. The details came flooding back to him in living color. He thought for a few minutes about denying the charges but knew they had caught him cold. Perhaps if he told the police what had happened, he could convince them it was an accident, and they would let him go.

As Scott was answering police questions, a clear picture of prior events emerged. Scott had been a fifteen-year-old living the good life near Gloucester. He was popular in school and had lots of friends. His father could afford to buy him nice things and surprised him with a Boston Whaler for his fifteenth birthday. He kept it at the dock of the family home in Beverly Farms.

On that fateful Sunday morning in September 1980, Scott had slammed the back door and left the house in a huff, having just had an argument with his mother over finishing his homework. He headed to the dock, got on his boat, and cast off, figuring he would just motor around for a while until his anger lessened. The more he thought about the argument, though, the angrier he became. His mother was the typical helicopter mom, always getting on his back about one thing or another. He hated it but couldn't figure out what to do. His older brother, Rob, had had the same experience. When Rob first went to college, their mom had insisted that he take a fax machine with him so he could send her his papers and she could edit them.

The sky was blue, the water was calm, and the day was unseasonably mild. Scott headed northeast toward Gloucester. Before he realized it, he was approaching Gloucester Harbor and decided to stop at Pier 7 to buy a soda or some ice cream.

As he docked the boat, he noticed a little girl standing there, looking upset. She told him she had been out for a bike ride and had gotten a flat tire from a splinter on the dock.

Scott's first thought was to offer to take the bike somewhere to get it fixed. For some inexplicable reason, he didn't do that. Rather, he asked her if she wanted to go for a boat ride. She said yes.

Scott and Maia headed out of the harbor. The swells were picking up, and at one point Scott gunned the engine to move the boat over an oncoming wave. Maia was standing in the bow. She lost her balance and fell, hitting her head hard on a conch shell that Scott had found on the beach and tossed into the boat.

Scott started to laugh until he realized how serious this was. He went to the bow to check on her but found that she was out cold and her head was bleeding profusely from the wound. He tried to revive her and couldn't. Scott knew a little CPR and tried it, but it didn't work. After she remained unresponsive for ten minutes, he concluded she must be dead.

That's when he freaked out.

"Oh my God, oh my God, oh my God. What should I do?"

He knew he should go right back to the dock and tell someone. But he was petrified. They'd want to know what he was doing out on the water alone with an eleven-year-old girl. He wasn't doing anything, but no one would believe him.

Certainly not his mother, who would ground him for a year. So he made the unfortunate decision to cover his tracks.

First, he motored to Ravenswood Park and dragged the body deep into the woods. He tried to cover it with dirt as best he could. He also tossed the conch shell as far as he could. His first thought had been to throw it overboard, but he thought it might float.

He had left Maia's backpack in his boat. After leaving Ravenswood, he motored over to Stage Fort Park and dropped off the backpack, thinking this could throw off investigators.

Finally, he headed home. At the dock, Scott scrubbed down the boat to remove any remaining evidence.

Scott was haunted by what had happened and thought about telling someone from time to time. But he could never bring himself to do it. And as more time passed, it became harder and harder to think about revealing his secret. Gradually, it just became part of who he was. He could put it in his basement and pretend it never happened.

Now, sitting in the police interrogation room, Scott was scared, but he also felt a sense of relief. He was genuinely remorseful about what he had done, and it now was out in the open. He would just have to wait and see what punishment the prosecutor would decide to impose.

In analyzing his DNA sample, the police had found that Scott's mother's maternal grandfather and Sylvia's paternal grandmother were brother and sister. Although they didn't know each other, Scott and Doron were second cousins once removed. Scott bore the same familial relationship to Mark and Ricky.

CHAPTER THIRTY-SIX

After the police called me in 2015, I started to mull over what I then knew. My DNA had been a match to two individuals, but I didn't know who they were or what side of my family they were on. Eventually, miscellaneous DNA matches began to appear on AncestryDNA. They were remote, however, and I couldn't figure out how to make use of the information. Carol Davis, for instance, was a third or fourth cousin, but the family tree that she had downloaded showed names I had never encountered before, and there was no one with Eisen as the last name. I was frustrated, to say the least.

The situation changed dramatically in 2018, when I received a notice from AncestryDNA informing me that I had a match to someone who was a half sibling. His name was Richard Finberg, and he lived in Boston. According to AncestryDNA, he and I shared 1,991 cMs, or 29 percent of our DNA. This amount of shared DNA meant he in fact was 8.5 cMs short of being a full brother. We were linked paternally.

Of course, I knew the name Finberg and knew that the family patriarch had died. Artem Finberg must have been my father. This was incredible! I immediately told Rachel, who was so pleased for me. I then reached out to Richard through the AncestryDNA website, since no address, phone number, or email address was provided. I wondered whether he went by the name Richard, Dick, Rich, or Ricky. Or maybe something altogether different.

I was nervous but also excited. My note, however, was unemotional. I told him I had learned from AncestryDNA that we were half brothers and assumed he had learned the same thing. I then said I hoped to have the opportunity to obtain information about my biological father and his family. If he were agreeable, I'd love to talk on the phone and perhaps meet in person. But if that made him uncomfortable, I would totally understand. He might not even have known I existed, I added, and so the news must have come as a shock. I gave him my email address and phone number so he could reply.

The next day, I received a nice email message. "Call me Ricky," he started out, adding that he didn't know much about his own extended family and had sent in a DNA sample to find out. Ricky told me he had two brothers, Mark and Doron, meaning I did as well. His father's name was Artem, and he had died some years ago, which I knew. His mother, Sylvia, had moved back to Brooklyn Heights, into the apartment she had inherited from her mother, and probably had no idea that Artem had fathered a child out of wedlock. This was during bachelorhood, Ricky said, when his father probably was just sowing his wild oats.

Ricky and I agreed to talk on the phone the following evening. He said he had told Mark and Doron about me. They were as shocked as he was to learn they had a half brother, but knowing their father, they thought it made sense. They held no ill will toward me but were not sure how they felt about talking or meeting. The one thing the three of them felt strongly was that their mother, Sylvia, should never be told. It would destroy her, they all believed.

When I said I, too, lived in the Boston area, Ricky immediately suggested that we get together. We met two days later for dinner at Joe's on Newbury, near Copley Square. I got there first, taking a seat looking out at the door so I could spot him. When he walked in, I could tell immediately that we were related. We had the same eyes and mouth.

He casually sauntered over to me, I stood up, and we checked each other out. We were almost like two cheetahs dancing around each other, gauging whether we were going to fight or embrace. He ended up embracing me, and I did the same to him.

"Wow," he said, "this is so unreal."

"It certainly is," I replied.

"When were you born?"

"In 1950." I outlined all that I knew—my mother was single, had gotten pregnant at a time when becoming pregnant before marriage was almost a sin. My mother couldn't take care of me on her own. Her own mother had died, and she couldn't live with a baby at her father's and stepmother's home in Brooklyn because she and her stepmother didn't get along. I was adopted when I was six months old by parents who loved me, and I had a good upbringing on Long Island. I also said I always knew I was adopted but that that didn't keep me from finding my biological roots.

"If you were born in 1950, that was right around the time that Dad shipped off for Korea. He was living in Brooklyn with his parents and was quite the ladies' man, based on his bragging over the years. My guess is he convinced some girl he knew or met to jump in the hay with him and you were the product."

"That makes sense," I said. "Tell me about yourself and your family."

"Well, in a nutshell, my parents grew up in Brooklyn, met each other in their twenties, and eventually moved to Gloucester after they got married. My father—I should say OUR father—operated a charter fishing company for many years. It was called Gloucester Sea Charter Outfitters—you may have heard of it."

"Yes, I have." I didn't think this was the time to tell him that I knew a lot about his family from the news.

"Well, to continue, our family is Jewish, although not terribly religious. Not any longer, at least. I have an older brother, Mark, and a younger brother, Doron. I was married for a couple of years but got divorced about two decades ago. The center of my life is my son, Hunter, now twenty-four, who now lives with me when he isn't running around somewhere else with his friends."

I told Ricky about my own family: my wife, Rachel; my daughter Amy and her husband Ken; and my other daughter Jocelyn and her husband Ethan. Neither had kids, I added.

"Could you tell me about your dad?" I continued. I was deliberate in not calling him "our" dad because even though I knew he was in a biological sense, Ricky had a much greater claim to him than I did.

"Well, he was kind to others and supportive of all three of his boys. He was a Scout leader. It was because of him that we learned survival tactics in the woods. I remember one time when he, Mark, and I went camping in Maine for the weekend. I must have been about twelve at the time. Our mother had packed enough food for us to cook over the campfire, but not much else to eat. We had canteens full of water and a large tent. When we arrived at a lake midafternoon, we immediately set about pitching the tent by the side of the beautiful lake. Right after that we jumped into the lake and started splashing around. Suddenly, we saw a black bear near us on shore. I'm not sure how large it was, but at the time it seemed enormous. He was standing erect, just staring at us. Suddenly, the bear entered the lake and started to swim toward us. I thought it was cute, but Dad was alarmed and told us to get back. We backed away from the bear slowly, and as we were doing so, Dad grabbed a dead branch that was floating nearby and started to thrust it at the bear, to scare the bear away. The trick didn't work, and the bear just kept coming nearer and nearer. We kept backing up in the same increments. Eventually, we were back on shore, and Dad started to pick up stones and hurl them at the bear. That seemed to do the trick, as the bear let out a big roar, turned, and started to walk away.

"We were safe, I thought, until we weren't. The bear must have sniffed our food because it suddenly started to saunter toward the tent, where the provisions were kept. Dad took a glowing stick from the campfire and threw it at the bear. It hit him in the chest, and some of its hair started on fire. The bear roared loudly, ran to the lake, and jumped in, dousing the fire in its chest hair. The bear left us alone after that.

"I have no idea if he acted appropriately," Ricky continued, "but it sure seemed right to me. Had Dad not done what he did, I might have been dead meat.

"I had a bar mitzvah when I was thirteen," Ricky said, "but did not do much in the religious realm after that. Dad, on the other hand, did, even though he told us he was not a true believer. He worked to support the temple by bringing in new members. He also had the reputation of being a pillar of the community. He was active in the local Rotary Club. He brought in many new club members and got lots of awards. Unfortunately, he died the year after 9/11, after having gone to New York with the Gloucester Volunteer Fire Department to help with the recovery efforts.

"Had you known him, you would have been proud of him. We all were. He was a stand-up guy. I'd bet he didn't even know you existed. If he had known about you, he would have acknowledged you and taken responsibility, for sure."

CHAPTER THIRTY-SEVEN

Ricky and I got together several more times. On one of those occasions, I tried to describe how emotionally grounded I'd felt after he told me about my father. It was and remains difficult to put this into words. Growing up, when I didn't know where I came from, biologically speaking, I always felt different from other people. Even if others had weird relatives, they at least knew who their ancestors were. Not having that information created a pit in my stomach—a cavernous void.

In elementary school I had a friend named Will whose parents seemed a bit arcane. They adhered to the principles of Christian Science, a nontraditional denomination of Christianity that strongly believes in the healing power of faith in Jesus. Will's mother, Bobbie, had attended a Seven Sisters college, and his father, Matt, had graduated from a New England Ivy League school. Higher education was rare in those days and available only to the rich, so I figured they were the product of America's upper crust. I later learned how wrong I was. Will's parents had both grown up in Jewish homes and converted, apparently, in part, to elude what they grasped as the stigma of being Jewish in America. Will's father worked for his father-in-law in the New York textile industry. Of the kids in the family, only Will's older sister had a close relationship with their paternal grandmother, Estelle, who ran a Brooklyn delicatessen and was proud of it. Will's sister moved to Europe to escape her parents and subsequently wrote about her difficulties growing up with her mother. According to what Will's sister wrote, Bobbie was extremely anti-Semitic and believed she had cleansed herself of her Judaic taint by converting. Eventually, mother and daughter decided to have nothing more to do with each other. Bobbie's obituary reported that she was the mother of (only) two sons.

I note this now because as a kid I was envious of Will for being a member of what seemed like a well-integrated biological family. In his family, I magically believed, parents would unconditionally shower love on their children for all eternity. Regarding myself as existentially different, I felt alone. Yes, I had parents who loved me very much. But rightly or wrongly, I believed that if I displeased them, I would be sent back to the adoption agency. The sword of Damocles was continually swaying overhead.

CHAPTER THIRTY-EIGHT

In our conversations, Ricky was forthcoming with me as well. He told me he was never close to his parents or brothers growing up. His parents provided guidance but not real love and affection. It was as if each person in the Finberg family was in an orbit of his or her own. Ricky's interest in learning more about his genealogy was piqued when he learned that he (as Doron's brother) was distantly related to the person who had killed Maia. Neither Mark nor Doron felt the same way. Mark's thinking was tainted by the fact that he had been an early suspect in Maia's disappearance. Doron, for his part, was still angry that his DNA was a partial match to that of the individual who had caused Maia's death. He wanted nothing more to do with DNA matches.

Ricky then continued to tell me his own narrative. He eventually decided he had had enough of Emmy's behavior and demanded a divorce. Under the prenup, he was not entitled to any of the Welds' family money, including the money in trust for Emily, but he didn't care. All he wanted was to start over. Emmy received full custody of their son, Hunter, under the divorce decree, but Ricky had him every other weekend. When

Artem and Sylvia were living in Gloucester, he would sometimes take Hunter to visit them. Artem was a doting grandfather, but Sylvia was more into her mah-jongg games than her only grandson.

Ricky had bought a small house in Lexington. He liked the outdoors and found the environment very calming.

Ricky spent considerable time filling me in on the actual details of our father's life. He told me that Artem had been a steward aboard *Andrea Doria*. At first reluctant, he eventually revealed that Artem had absconded with Ruth Roman's jewels and later sold them to buy Gloucester Sea Charter Outfitters. Ricky wasn't sure that Artem was aware that Ricky knew that; he had learned it as a teen when he'd overheard a heated argument between Artem and Sylvia.

On one of the last times that Ricky and I got together, he opened up about a lot of personal things despite our fifteen-year age difference. Or perhaps it was the age difference that made things easier for him.

"You know I went to MIT," he said as a statement rather than a question. "I was a serious student and did well there, but I also didn't have much of a life. I was in Zeta Beta Tau, the Jewish fraternity founded in 1898, but it had a considerably Asian composition when I was there. I did go to dances and other social events, but still felt as though I missed out on a true college experience.

"Anyway," Ricky continued, "after I graduated and located a job, I was bursting at the seams to have some fun. I would go to local bars after work and on the weekends and meet girls. We often hooked up, but they weren't marrying material. Most were from local junior colleges and didn't have intellectual streaks. I wanted an intellectual connection as well as a physical one. Then I met my future wife, Emmy. We connected on so many levels. I'm a little embarrassed to say this, but she also came from a rich and prominent family, the Welds. She was fun and funny. She swept me off my feet. I wasn't sure our families would mesh. They never became close, but they were genuinely cordial. Emmy's mother even danced the hora at our wedding."

"So what happened?" I asked.

"Well, once we were married, Emmy completely changed. Her materialistic side began to dwarf her easygoing, fun-loving side. Even though her family had money, she didn't personally, except in her untouchable trust fund, and she kept wanting more and more expensive things. Then she became pregnant. I was overjoyed about having a child, but I also felt cornered. Even though I earned a fine living at AI Squared, how would I ever satisfy her needs?"

"It sounds a little bit like me," I said. "I was always trying to please my parents."

"That's an interesting comparison," Ricky offered with some annoyance. "Turning back to me…I did something quite stupid. I contacted this guy Griffin, who was somehow related to Emmy. He was a real mover and had promised me a job. I knew he was into something illegal but wasn't sure what. He offered me a boatload of money if I arranged to use one of Dad's boats at night to shuttle between Gloucester Harbor and a ship passing in the Atlantic, and that's what I did. As it turns out, he was picking up drugs. The Coast Guard seized the ship and arrested Griffin and my brother Doron, who was at the helm. Doron went to prison for me."

All I could say was "Wow." Then I asked if he had apologized to Doron, and he said no.

"You really should," I replied.

"I know…I will."

It was hard for me to take this all in. I told him I needed to get going but suggested that we get together again the following week.

CHAPTER THIRTY-NINE

At a bar the following Thursday evening, Ricky told me he had called Doron and invited him over for a beer. In his living room, with his own beer in hand to make the conversation easier, Ricky brought up Doron's incarceration, saying that he felt responsible.

"It's not your fault," Doron said.

"Actually, it is," Ricky responded, "because I was the one who suggested you operate the nighttime charters."

"Nah, you didn't know what Griffin was up to."

Ricky was silent for a full minute, knowing that Doron didn't always piece information together as well as others.

"Listen, Doron," Ricky said. "I know you think that, but I had an inkling that something illegal was going on because I was paid extra by Griffin. That's how I was able to give you the extra $3,000 per trip."

Apparently, Ricky didn't have it in him to tell Doron the truth, the whole truth, and nothing but the truth, which was that Ricky would have been an idiot not to know that drugs were involved.

"Would you like to meet Hunter?" Ricky then asked me. I told him I would love to and suggested that he and Hunter come over for dinner the following Saturday. Ricky said yes tentatively; he would need to check with Hunter, who had an active social calendar. When Ricky asked Hunter, the immediate response was a yes.

Before coming over, Ricky told Hunter that I was his uncle. He also revealed some of my circumstances. I was curious to see if Hunter would be interested in hearing about my birth and adoption. He was, and I told him what I knew. He showed intellectual curiosity, not a desire for a connection at an emotional level. Still, Hunter and I hit it off right away, as new acquaintances might. We grilled hamburgers in the backyard and afterward melted marshmallows for s'mores. He was intrigued by my collection of model boats, especially the sailboat Jocelyn had bought for me from a model boat builder in Bequia, an island in St. Vincent and the Grenadines, where we had gone together on a sailing trip. Hunter also seemed to like Rachel a lot.

After that visit, Ricky and I just seemed to drift away from each other. Even though he wasn't close to his brothers, I think he still felt closer to them than he did to me. That became even more so as Sylvia started to age and need physical and emotional support from her boys. I never felt as though I were one of the Finberg brothers, but that is all right. I understood that, for them, finding a new half brother was a novelty, and perhaps even extraordinary. That is a far cry from being excited about welcoming a newly acquired relative into the family.

I believe Ricky and I both were aware that our connection was fading. We had started by being supportive of each other when we were speaking about our pasts. Technically, we also shared a father in common. However, having the same biological father did not turn us into true brothers, even though we now had a definitive genetic link. Ricky remembered the father who had raised him and his brothers. I had never even met the individual who had passed along his portion of my DNA to my biological mother.

CHAPTER FORTY

Having information about my biological father, I reminded myself, was only one piece of the equation. I wanted to dig further into my genetic roots and hopefully identify my mother. That could be an even more fruitful source of emotional clarity, I thought. I wondered whether my mother was still alive. According to the information I had received from Louise Wise, she was twenty years old at the time I was born, meaning she would be in her late eighties today. I also wanted to understand the circumstances of my conception, birth, and adoption placement. Where had my biological mother lived, I wondered? How had my parents met? Might I have any other siblings? If so, would they welcome me into the family fold? How would I react? Would the experience be like my experience meeting Ricky? No, it probably would be more intense, I thought. For some inexplicable reason, my maternal connections felt even more inflamed than my paternal connections.

I had occasionally watched several overly sentimental television series about people yearning to find their elusive biological families, being successful, and having mind-blowing experiences. In those shows, birth mothers and children would run toward each other and hug in long, tearful embraces. They would feel immediate emotional connections expected to remain in place for a lifetime. Would I have that experience? Probably not, I thought. It was ridiculous to believe that was the norm in real life. Still, I wanted to find out about my biological mother and her relatives. At a minimum, this would answer questions I'd harbored throughout my life. And I knew from Louise Wise that my maternal grandmother had died of cancer at age thirty-eight. Perhaps I would be able to obtain useful medical information.

At one point during my search, I had learned of the daughter of a family friend who had been successful in finding her own biological parents. She even wrote a book about it. When her mother had become pregnant, she was not ready to raise a child, and she and the father were not ready to get married, so their daughter was placed with an adoptive family. Remarkably, her parents did get married and had several more children. The adoptive daughter eventually found and met her mother, who brought her into the family. It must have been pure bliss, I thought. What I learned later in the book was that, for her, the electricity of the moment diminished in strength over time. She remained in touch with her biological family, but the connection was not the same as it once had been.

I did not allow any of these musings to take over my life. In fact, after a while I barely thought about the fact that my DNA was still on file with AncestryDNA and could produce a maternal match.

Then, one day, I was sitting in our family room going through emails on my laptop. It is amazing just how many emails come in each day. I was almost like a robot, pressing the Delete key repeatedly without reading the emails. I came to one from AncestryDNA and almost deleted it, too. "Ishmael, you have a new DNA match to explore," the subject line said.

My guess was that this was just another third, fourth, or even more distant cousin. I had found a lot of those and never been able to connect them to my more immediate family.

When I opened the email and logged into Ancestry.com, I saw that this new match was a second cousin named Jacob Goldstein, the closest relative I had found since matching with Ricky.

I contacted Jacob through AncestryDNA, and we exchanged personal email addresses. He had already identified his biological mother, who had died years earlier, and was searching for his father. His friend Joe, an amateur genealogist, was helping him. Together, they were navigating the complexities of GEDmatch, a database to which the user uploads DNA test results. Once that has been done, GEDmatch conducts a chromosome-by-chromosome comparison to identify similarities.

Eventually, GEDmatch confirmed what I had suspected—that Jacob and I were related through his father and my mother. He put the pieces together and determined that his paternal grandfather and my maternal grandfather had been brothers. He also identified several shared living relatives whom we both contacted. They provided a wealth of helpful information.

Jacob's story was quite like mine. His father had dated his mother for a while but was only in the relationship for the good times. A member of the Jewish Mafia in Miami, he had no interest in getting married and disappeared immediately after learning that Jacob's mother was pregnant. She did what any Jewish girl in her predicament would have done at the time: she asked her rabbi for help. He referred her to Louise Wise Services, the leading Jewish adoption agency in New York City, through which I also was adopted. Jacob shared an old photograph of Lakeview, the home for unwed mothers in Staten Island where our mothers were housed before giving birth. We also were born in the same Staten Island hospital.

One second cousin, Barbara, whom we shared, eagerly engaged with each of us. As I would come to learn, Barbara's immediate family was at the center of all things Ishmael.

Barbara's grandfather and mine were part of a large Jewish family that had emigrated from Ukraine in the early 1900s. Processed through Ellis Island, most went to live in Brooklyn. Barbara's grandfather (my great-uncle) was the outlier. He relocated to Rockland, Maine, in the Midcoast region, where he made his living selling secondhand goods to neighbors from a horse-drawn cart. My biological mother, Sophie, had grown up in Brooklyn with two older brothers and one younger sister. Neither Sophie nor either of her siblings was still living.

At that point I was sure that my story and Jacob's would follow the same trajectory, producing the well-known cliché: boy encounters girl, who gets pregnant and leaves the family home in shame to give birth somewhere else and give the child up for adoption. As it turned out, my situation was a bit more complicated.

When Sophie was two years old, she contracted scarlet fever, which, according to her family, impacted her cognitive development. Growing up, she had an engaging disposition but difficulty comprehending things. Following Sophie's mother's death, her father remarried, and the woman he selected lacked maternal instincts. She had little time for, and little interest in, her new stepdaughter. Sophie made it through high school with a lot of academic help along the way. However, her family didn't know how to plan her future. Sophie spent hours at home alone while her father was at work and her stepmother was absent. In nice weather, Sophie would sit on the front porch, shouting friendly greetings to boys in the neighborhood. Picture this: my mother says hi, invites a boy into the house, and, well, you can imagine the rest.

After learning the identities of my biological mother and father, I looked for their addresses in the 1940 US census. I knew that both had lived in Brooklyn, which was a good start. What I learned from the census was that my mother's and father's families had lived a block from each other. In other words, Artem Finberg was one of the neighborhood boys.

At that time, it was no big deal from the boy's point of view if he got a girl pregnant. That was just one example of guys being guys. The girl, however, had things much tougher, even if she, too, had enjoyed the encounter or encounters. She likely would need to tell her parents and then carry the baby to term. Usually this would be at a home for unwed mothers. She would disappear from the neighborhood. Friends and family would be told a lie—for example, that the mother had gone away for several months to live with an aunt. Once the baby was born, he or she would be put up for adoption. If the mother expressed interest in keeping the child, the adoption agency would exert maximum pressure on the girl and her family to ensure that that didn't happen.

It was difficult to process all this information. My birth mother and father were dead, I had no maternal siblings, and I didn't feel especially close to my paternal half brothers. On the other hand, I knew where I came from—a Jewish family with strong roots in Ukraine and widespread subsequent growth in the United States. I'd obtained important information, learning that my biological maternal grandmother had died from cancer at the age of thirty-eight and that my own mother had died from the same thing in her early seventies. That ought to be enough, I thought.

I was blown away several months later when my new cousin, Barbara, invited me to a combined family reunion and fiftieth-anniversary party she was planning in Maine. Rachel and I decided to go, joining about eighty other relatives and Maine neighbors. Held outside on a patio at a resort overlooking the Atlantic, the party was spectacular. Everyone had heard about me and was effusive. I felt welcomed and included. I was able to meet my mother's ninety-seven-year-old cousin, Ella, who still lived in Rockland in the same house in which she had lived as a child. This was near the family home that my mother and her siblings had stayed in each summer when escaping the Brooklyn heat. Ella was able to tell me stories about my mother as a child. Ella and her siblings had taken my mother under their wing.

What conceivably could be better, I had thought, than to find my place in a new, loving family, all members of which would embrace me just for being me? That's what happens on television reality shows about adoptees finding their birth families, after all. I now realize that is a pipe dream for many, including me.

I concluded it was enough just to find out about my birth and my parentage. Knowing that my birth mother had been incapable of being nurturing in the normal sense left me a bit forlorn, personally, as well as sad for her. But I knew she would have wanted to keep me if she had been able to raise me, and I also had adoptive parents who loved me dearly.

I was also happy to learn about my birth father and his shenanigans. It put my existence into perspective. I'd received 3,400 centimorgans of DNA from him, after all.

Pinpointing my birth parents and fleshing out their family stories has provided the impetus to accept that I have an authentic inscription in what Jews refer to as the Book of Life. The challenge is to keep that thought at the top of mind, which I sometimes can do by listening to music. Whether composed by Berlioz or the Beatles, a good tune carries me to a space where things are good and I belong.

Take the song "Hallelujah," written by Leonard Cohen in 1984, which combines a simple melody and haunting lyrics to produce a vibrant elegy of sorts about the human condition. Not everything we do is good and not all our decisions are the best ones. But those are all part of the voyage that is life.

To quote verse four from the original version of what is my favorite song:[10]

Now I've done my best, I know it wasn't much

I couldn't feel, so I tried to touch

I've told the truth, I didn't come here to fool ya

And even though it all went wrong

I'll stand right here before the lord of song

With nothing, nothing on my tongue but Hallelujah

CHAPTER FORTY-ONE

Life has a habit of moving on, whether you want it to or not. At the end of 2020, after I turned seventy, I was required to retire from the law firm. That was because of an ironclad firm policy, not because anyone thought I was slowing down or showing declining mental prowess. The firm's mandatory retirement policy was on the liberal side. Some firms mandate retirement at age sixty-five. From an economic standpoint, the policy makes perfect sense. Large law firms, at least, are through a flow-down model. The partner pool is relatively small. Partners are expected to bring in business through their professional or social connections. If they don't, they are penalized monetarily. They can do some of the work they bring in, but most is supposed to be assigned to the firm's large cadre of associates and special counsel, whose billing rates are touted as more "economical." I have put that word in quotes because there is something farcical about applying it to associate rates in the high triple digits and partner rates (like mine) exceeding $1,000 per hour. The billed hours produce sizable profits, which are distributed to the associates and counsel, in part, but predominantly to the partners. At a certain age, the partner must move aside to increase the profit pool for younger partners.

This model engenders a lot of internal competition between partners, between associates, and between partners and associates. Some would say the environment is cutthroat. Lawyers assist one another where absolutely necessary, but not without securing a cut of the work-related revenues. I hated the system but was able to compartmentalize it mostly successfully. Although I was at the lower end of the partner pecking order, I could live quite nicely on my compensation, which was low compared to that of other partners but plentiful in comparison to that of the population at large.

One thing I'll say about our firm and many others is that they attract a lot of egotistical people, each trying as hard as possible to climb to the top of the pecking order. Each would strive to be the top-billing partner, instantly gaining respect from others in the group. Following the end of each year, the managing partner compiled a table of the compensation of all partners and circulated it to the other partners. If you earned $5 million, your standing was much better than if you earned a "mere" $1 million. There were partner dinners and partner retreats, ostensibly designed to facilitate discussions about attracting more business but, in reality, gatherings at which to show off your wealth and social status. You might introduce a new girlfriend, boyfriend, or spouse, or showcase a Rolex or new piece of jewelry. Rachel kept telling me I should look for a different work environment, and she probably was right. But I was fearful of stirring the pot and venturing into something unfamiliar, so I never did.

Nevertheless, my years at the firm, by and large, were satisfying. I generally enjoyed my work. Specializing in ship financing and international maritime law, I was able to take frequent foreign trips, which I loved. On one occasion, the general counsel of one of our Netherlands clients asked me to accompany him to a conference at the Organization for Economic Development and Cooperation in Paris. He asked if my wife would consider joining me, as his own wife was going and wanted a companion for her shopping escapades. Rachel always loved to hunt for bargains. It was not easy for her to take time off from school, so she laid out the proposition to her principal gently. He responded, "What, are you crazy? Let's ask our genie. Paris or the Fuller School? Which will it be? It's Paris, of course. If you don't go on the trip, I'll go with Ish and even share a bed, if necessary."

By far the hardest part of practicing law was having to deal with the political types in the firm's Washington, DC, office. They were always organizing one campaign fundraiser or another for some US senator or congressman funded by handouts from people at the firm. These events were coordinated by the firm's political action committee (the "PAC"), which had a well-honed apparatus for extracting contributions to the maximum extent permitted by law. Late each year, the PAC board would meet and set the coming year's budget, which included the projected inflow and outflow of funds. Suggested amounts were set for individual lawyers as a percentage of their compensation, up to the statutory maximum of $5,000 per election. As required by law, contributions were ostensibly voluntary. But when someone from firm management came to your office and asked you to sign up, it was hard to say no. Once you signed the form given to you, the pro rata share of the annual amount would be deducted from each future paycheck.

Like other US law firms wishing to punch above their weight, we had opened a DC office and a PAC to advance our clients' legislative interests. For instance, prior to the 1998 settlement between consumers and the major US tobacco companies, our firm represented several US companies opposed to the draconian measures then being advanced in Congress. I was involved in legislative matters only occasionally, such as when the US Export-Import Bank was up for reauthorization or the Jones Act came under review. Also known as the Merchant Marine Act of 1920, the Jones Act was passed after World War I to encourage the development and maintenance of a US merchant shipping fleet. The act provided this encouragement by prohibiting foreign vessels from carrying cargo from one US port to another except in limited circumstances key to the national defense. As a result of the Jones Act, no foreign vessel may carry goods from the US mainland to Puerto Rico, for example, or vice versa. The impact is substantial because the US merchant fleet has been declining in size and now stands below two hundred vessels, less than 1 percent of the global merchant fleet.

Unless one knows senators and congressmen or people who work for them, it is not easy to gain access to the Capitol Hill inner sanctum. Legal prohibitions against gifts are strict, so the best way to gain access is through the campaign contribution process. If someone promises to present a large check from a PAC and/or individual donors, politicians listen. Campaign contributions, of course, cannot be used to influence votes or to secure support on matters of public interest. However, as our nation's political leadership is quick to point out, the possibility of corruption is not of concern because elected officials would never entertain the thought of deciding a legislative matter on the basis of a campaign contribution or personal relationship!

Lest anyone have the notion that campaign contributions are inconsequential, think again. An organization called "Open Secrets" tracks congressional contributions and expenditures, which must be reported to the Federal Election Commission. In the 2019–2020 election cycle, the top Senate fundraiser was Senator Tim Scott, Republican from South Carolina and minority member of the Senate Banking Committee, who raised a total of $42.4 million, including $3.5 million in PAC contributions. On the House side, Minority Leader Kevin McCarthy topped the fundraising list, taking in $19.3 million in contributions, including $768,000 in PAC money. Compare this to the scenario in the United Kingdom, where campaign expenditures are legally capped at £30,000 per candidate per election.

At our firm, the PAC was run with an iron fist by Éléanor Nevermore, an outwardly demure lobbyist with a sweet-as-sugar facade and a heart of stone. She was married to Brandon Nevermore, a Louisiana-born-and-breed lobbyist working for the nuclear power industry. They had met ten-or-so years earlier at a Democratic Party fundraiser at the Greenbrier, a West Virginia resort offering horse riding, tennis, skeet shooting, spa treatments, and, of most interest to the couple, "Bourbon at the Bar." Fortunately, because I am based in Boston and don't regularly become involved in congressional matters, I had limited contact with her. From what I understand, she had successfully inveigled herself into the hearts and minds of those who ran the firm and made the compensation decisions. For instance, through her Democratic Party connections, she knew a high-ranking member of the House of Representatives from California, whose district was where one of the firm's large clients was based. It made perfect sense to direct PAC contributions to him, and Éléanor did so regularly. She also once arranged a small dinner for the client's CEO and the member. Afterward, senior firm management crowed that Éléanor had hit a home run and promptly sponsored a follow-up fundraiser for the member. The member had suggested a $50,000 fundraising goal, which was easily exceeded. I was asked to contribute $1,000, which I felt obligated to do to avoid an unspoken black mark in the firm's compensation process. Those with more gravitas contributed willingly, judging (correctly) that they would more than make up for it at the end of the year, when the success of the PAC had been demonstrated and law firm bonuses were awarded. I, on the other hand, feared if I didn't contribute to the PAC at the recommended level, my bonus would be reduced.

Like many of her political friends, Éléanor lived on the edge of the law. When Senator McCain supported amending the Jones Act to expand interstate shipping opportunities by foreign ship owners, she asked me if I would be interested in sponsoring a fundraiser for the senator and inviting my foreign clients. When I asked if that was permissible, she told me not to worry about it because I am a US citizen and contributions from foreign clients could be channeled through their US subsidiaries. Perhaps that was correct, but I didn't feel comfortable with that advice.

A piece of work, Éléanor was sometimes referred to behind her back as Her Highness or simply Raven. She had a pillow in her office inscribed "Queen of Virtually Everything," which she told people a friend had given her as a gag gift. I wonder. Éléanor was known to speak badly of colleagues and claimed credit for having driven out the partner who recruited her to the firm.

From time to time, Éléanor also liked to joke that her paternal ancestors came from Corsica, birthplace of Napoleon, where people held exceptionally long grudges (and she did too). "So watch out," she would say, with a wide grin disguising the true meaning of her words.

The end came abruptly for Éléanor in 2022, after I had retired from the firm. As some may recall, 2020 was an interesting year. The COVID-19 pandemic hit with a vengeance, many people abhorred the idea of taking a vaccine, and the then US president suggested that a better antidote might be to inject bleach into one's veins. The economy was suffering. In January 2021, Congress made billions of dollars available in direct grants, loans, and loan guarantees to essential businesses affected by the pandemic. One category was the US defense industry. Éléanor handled Washington, DC, representation for a firm client, a Boston-based defense contractor, that qualified for loan guarantees. At Éléanor's recommendation, the company applied for and was awarded a loan guarantee totaling $75 million. To receive the funds, the client had to provide financial records and certain legal assurances about use of the loan proceeds. The client provided those records and assurances, and it received the loan guarantee. It took the inspector general of the US Department of the Treasury almost two years to complete an audit, but he finally did so in 2022, finding that the company had violated the assurances when it used federally-guaranteed loan proceeds to build a home office addition for the CEO at his Cape Cod beach house and to lease a fleet of new Cadillac Escalades for its cadre of executives. The inspector general referred the matter to the US Department of Justice, which decided to indict the company, its CEO, its CFO, and its general counsel. Éléanor was fortunate to avoid indictment based on her own involvement. She had vetted the question of loan proceed use with several members of Congress, who told her not to worry because, when drafting the legislation, they had meant for courts to apply a loose reading of the legal assurances. The US attorney overseeing the case did not think that reading was reasonable, however, and argued in the court proceeding that the defendants violated the law's clear intent to prevent unjust enrichment of top executives.

Éléanor used her Democratic Party connections to find the best criminal defense attorney to represent the company and its indicted executives. She identified just the right attorney, a partner of the Washington, DC, office of a Democratic-leaning, Texas-based firm with connections to Big Oil. The partner agreed to put his top associates on the case, billing them at the blended rate of a mere $1,100 per hour. Unfortunately, the law firm team concluded that the defendants lacked credible cases. With the defendants' reluctant consent, the firm reached out to the US attorney's office about a plea deal. After some back and forth, the company agreed to plead guilty to multiple counts and to pay a fine of $10 million. Each individual defendant agreed to plead guilty to a single count—the misappropriation of government funds in violation of 18 U.S.C. 644. Each also agreed to accept a fine of $10,000, and a suspended sentence of one year's jail time.

Shortly after that occurred, the company fired its CEO, CFO, and general counsel, and switched its government affairs representation to another firm. Éléanor's standing at our firm wilted, and firm management counseled her to take an unpaid leave of absence while she explored other professional opportunities. After job searching for six months, Éléanor was lucky to land a mid-level position in the Washington, DC, office of Planned Parenthood.

CHAPTER FORTY-TWO

On June 20, 2023, I spent a quiet day on my sailboat in Gloucester Harbor, cleaning the cockpit and replacing a few worn fittings. It was five years since I had learned who my birth father and half brothers were, four years since I'd identified my birth mother and her family, and more than two years since I'd retired.

The sailboat was new—or rather, a used boat but new to me. After years of putting off getting a boat because Rachel easily got seasick, didn't do well with the patch, and was scared she would get sick if she tried taking motion sickness tablets, as several of her friends had suggested, I decided to take the leap. I was feeling reflective and acknowledged it was a purchase I should have made long before. The boat was a Catalina 275, three years old and twenty-six feet in length, with a nice cockpit for day sailing and a small cabin for overnighting.

On the boat and more generally in retirement, I had a lot of time to think and discover. One topic to which I kept returning was the derivation of my name, Ishmael. Did my parents just like it? Was I named Ishmael after the narrator in *Moby-Dick*, one of my father's favorites?

I reminded myself how lucky I had been. I still had a loving marriage, albeit one with discouraging challenges early on. But hey, that's not unusual, right? And I should take pride in my ability to overcome those challenges (much to my parents' dismay) with our marriage still intact. I had raised two great kids, who now had successful careers and happy marriages of their own. Neither has children, which saddens me because I would love to be a doting grandfather like most of my peers. But that's not in my wheelhouse to fix.

When I identified both of my biological families, I was ecstatic—and relieved. For the first time in a long time, if ever, I felt truly at peace. I grasped that I was like everyone else, an integral part of a family with a history, rather than, in my mind, having been left shortly after birth on the side of the road to be picked up by the first passing Samaritan. But those feelings have faded over time. I am still grateful to know about my past, but I never became close with my new half brothers, who had a totally different upbringing. That's OK—really.

It now feels more certain than ever that I was not a stray abandoned at the side of the road. I feel much more whole than I did before. Still, beliefs imprinted early in life are not easy to cast aside. Sometimes the old ones reemerge. When they do, I try to move around them by acknowledging their origin and authenticity.

Recently, for example, as I was nearing the end of this tale, I had a murky dream in which I was roaming around a ship on which I knew no one. I kept taking new passageways but could not find anyone with whom to speak. Eventually, I ran into my father, Edgar, who barely recognized or acknowledged me.

After uttering a muted hello, he said he had just bought a small boat for a young man he recently had befriended. I had no idea who the guy was and sensed that my father was thankful to have found someone to take my place.

Through this expression of the emotional impact of my adoption, I can almost hear my long-dead parents berating me for being a wimp and spewing nonsense. "Brooding about your birth parents is ridiculous," they might say. "We are your parents, and that should be good enough." In my cerebral response, I reject their thinking. It is distinct from and damaging to my own psyche.

CHAPTER FORTY-THREE

When someone retires, he or she looks for new interests. One of mine was checking on sales at Sotheby's auction house, a well-known purveyor of art, jewelry, and other fine items in New York City for the rich and famous. I signed up to receive emails from Sotheby's and obtain them at least weekly about upcoming events.

Recently, one of the emails announced the upcoming auction of opulent jewelry. I rarely pay attention because the pieces are so highly priced, and who would want to wear them anyway in today's informal social environment? On this day, however, I decided to open the email and examine the contents. It called the reader's attention to the offering of "magnificent jewels." I scrolled through the lots and fixated on one elegant offering. Showing a required opening bid of $850,000, it featured a color photograph of a set of diamond-and-sapphire earrings, each with three hanging pendants. Someone had already placed a bid of $875,000. I was stunned. All I could do was stare at the auction entry. The earrings were beautiful, yes, but, somehow, they also looked familiar. As I sat at the computer, I remembered having searched for information about Ruth

Roman a year or two earlier, after learning of her connection to Artem Finberg. I had come across a dazzling photograph of Ms. Roman in a red dress and earrings that looked remarkably like those in the Sotheby's online catalogue. Could the earrings in the Sotheby's lot be Ruth Roman's?

They certainly could, I thought. Or perhaps two sets of identical earrings had been made. That was possible but seemed improbable. Should I click on the Sotheby's website link for more information? I pondered. How could I not? After all, the jewels were part of my ancestry, metaphorically speaking.

After I clicked on the link, the following lot description appeared:

> A pair of ear clips made by Cartier, each one centering on an emerald-cut sapphire weighing 8.58 carats, framed and accented by round diamonds, size 6 ¼, with three diamond-studded pendants, having lengths of 2 ½ inches, 3 inches, and 3 ½ inches, respectively, each adorned at the bottom with a circular cluster of diamonds and sapphires. Diamonds, weighing a total of approximately 53.3 carats, are approximately F–G color, primarily VS clarity, with a few SI clarity examples. Sapphires in pendant clusters total approximately 17.3 carats. Signed Cartier Paris, with French assay marks.

These must be Ruth Roman's earrings, I thought. No doubt about it. What do I do now? I realize that question may not be on most people's radar, but for me, it was real. Legal ownership of the earrings could be uncertain.

My mind went into overdrive thinking about the various possible legal permutations, and I did some research. Under standard auction procedures, Sotheby's signs two contracts, one with the seller and one with the purchaser. In the former, the seller warrants that it holds valid legal ownership of the lot item. In the latter, Sotheby's gives the buyer the right to return the item and secure a refund from Sotheby's if the buyer finds that the ownership interest that passed from the seller to the buyer is invalid or of questionable validity. In a similar case in the United Kingdom, *Sotheby's v. Mark Weiss Ltd.*, Sotheby's had refunded the purchase price of a $10 million painting to a buyer who had come forward with information that called the authenticity of the painting into question. Sotheby's sued one of the sellers to recover the purchase price and was successful.

I thought of informing Sotheby's that the earrings had belonged to Ruth Roman and been pocketed by a ship employee before he jumped into a lifeboat from *Andrea Doria*. What would Sotheby's do then? It would probably cancel the auction, thus sidestepping the situation in which it had found itself in *Sotheby's v. Mark Weiss Ltd.* The seller then would have to figure out another way to sell the jewels if it could.

Another possibility would be to inform Ricky and ask what he thought I should I do. He would have been concerned about my doing anything to risk tainting the Finberg name. Keep quiet, he would have told me. Knowing that, I wondered what the point would be of telling him about my discovery.

The easiest and most obvious choice was to remain silent. Was that fair to the ultimate purchaser? Probably not, I concluded, because validity of title could be challenged if knowledge of Ruth Roman's prior ownership ever came to light. Yet I didn't even know who the purchaser would be. Perhaps this potential harm was too remote to consider.

In a surprise even to myself, I thought of Éléanor Nevermore, wondering what she would do in the same situation. One of her vocations was to absolve others of accountability in messy situations. If I had asked her, she would have said, "If it isn't broken, don't try to fix it," or in other words, keep your big mouth shut. I also thought about what Artem would have done and concluded that he, too, would have kept quiet and stayed out of the headlights. So that is what I did—I zipped my lips and didn't mention what I had found to a single soul. As the saying goes, at least in that respect, "Like father, like son."

CHAPTER FORTY-FOUR

Well, it is almost time for the fat lady to sing her aria. I do not know whether she will praise or scold me for embarking on the quest to find my biological roots. Perhaps she will term it a slap in the face of my mother Joan, who throughout her life embraced the magical thought that I was the product of her womb. Perhaps she will dub it an intrusion into the life of my biological father and his immediate family, of which I was not meant to be a part. Or, alternatively, perhaps she will scoff at my not trying to involve myself in the ongoing dynamics of that family.

I prefer to think of this journey as my birthright, which I alone have been afforded the capacity to navigate. The storms and swells encountered during the voyage are part of my own human fabric.

As aptly stated in another verse of Leonard Cohen's "Hallelujah":

> You say I took the name in vain
>
> I don't even know the name

But if I did, well, really, what's it to you?

There's a blaze of light in every word

It doesn't matter which you heard

The holy or the broken Hallelujah

The End

EPILOGUE

Did Louise Wise Services bear responsibility for deficient placement practices? Upon reflection, I believe the answer must be yes.

At the time of my adoption and for several later decades, Louise Wise was the preeminent Jewish adoption agency in New York City, if not the entire country. Successor to the Child Adoption Agency founded in 1916 by Louise Wise and her husband, Rabbi Stephen Wise, it regularly paired childless Jewish couples with Jewish children of unwed mothers. Its stated objective was to use a scientific approach in pairing couples and children that would be most compatible. However, there was nothing scientific about the process that was followed.

"Premium parents deserved premium babies, while ordinary parents were best paired with ordinary children," writes Gabrielle Glaser in her book, *American Baby*, about Louise Wise adoptions in the late 1940s and beyond.[11] The agency used various untested and spurious techniques to assess the intellectual capabilities of infants and to match them to so-called blue-ribbon families.[12]

Louise Wise Services also made experimental placements to obtain scientific data for use in the "nature versus nurture" debate. The issue raised was whether genetics or environmental factors played more of a role in influencing child development. In a memoir, two identical twins, Elyse Schein and Paula Bernstein, tell the story of how they were separated at birth by Louise Wise and placed with different families to facilitate a "nature versus nurture" study.[13] Neither the birth mother nor the adoptive parents knew that the study was occurring. According to the literature, that type of thing happened on multiple occasions.[14]

Similarly, a film documentary, *Three Identical Strangers*, tells the incredible story of identical triplets separated at birth so Louise Wise Services could engage in another similar study. As in other examples, each triplet had no knowledge that the others existed. The birth mother did not know. Nor were the three sets of adoptive parents made aware. The situation came to light only after one of the triplets was thought to be another at the State University of New York.[15]

In *American Baby*, Gabrielle Glaser describes other viscerally unacceptable practices designed to pressure young unwed women to give up children for adoption in situations where they wanted to keep their babies.[16] For instance, Louise Wise coerced signatures on consent forms and prevented mothers from seeing or bonding with their babies. As it did so, it was acting in the belief that satisfying the demand of childless Jewish couples was more important than responding to the entreaties of birth mothers to keep and raise their children. The best interest of the child appears to have been scarcely considered, even though internal agency documents termed an adoption "a major human event" and the child's ensuing transfer to new parents "a crisis with enduring consequences."[17]

Equally troublesome was the practice of fictionalizing or sanitizing information given to adoptive couples about the birth mothers and their families to elevate the child's "credentials" or to hide a history of mental illness, which was not considered genetically inheritable at the time.[18] In the response from Louise Wise to my request for information about my birth mother, I learned only that she was unmarried and unable to care for me—not that she suffered from cognitive difficulties. Given that present knowledge and the agency's practice of hiding information about mental impediments within birth families, I am nearly certain my adoptive parents were never informed either. Had they been, it is anyone's guess what they would have done.

ENDNOTES

1. Pierette Domenica Simpson, *Alive on the* Andrea Doria*!: The Greatest Sea Rescue in History* (Garden City, NY: Morgan James Publishing, 2008), 35.
2. Ibid.
3. Ibid., 36.
4. Ibid., 224.
5. Information about the *Andrea Doria* and its fateful last journey was obtained from various public sources, including *Alive on the* Andrea Doria*!*, Greg King and Penny Wilson, *The Last Voyage of the* Andrea Doria*: The Sinking of the World's Most Glamorous Ship* (New York: St. Martin's Press, 2000), and Richard Goldstein, *Desperate Hours: The Epic Rescue of the* Andrea Doria (New York: Wiley, 2001).
6. Our Wicked Fish, Inc., "Which New England Fish Are in Season," 2024, ourwickedfish.com/local-in-season-seafood-new-england.
7. US National Science Foundation, "Overfishing Linked To Rapid Evolution of Codfish," July 11, 2023, new.nsf.gov/news/overfishing-linked-rapid-evolution-codfish.

8. "CommonWealth Staff, "They That Go Down to the Sea in Ships," *CommonWealth Beacon*, December 6, 2017, commonwealthbeacon.org/the-download/go-sea-ships/.

9. James Taylor, vocalist, "Sweet Baby James," Track 2 on *Sweet Baby James*, LP Album, Warner Bros. Records, Released February 1, 1970.

10. Leonard Cohen, vocalist, "Hallelujah," Track 5 on *Various Positions*, LP Album, Columbia Records (Canada), Released December 11, 1984.

11. Gabrielle Glaser, *American Baby: A Mother, a Child, and the Shadow History of Adoption* (New York: Penguin Random House, 2021), 96.

12. Ibid., 96–102.

13. Paula Bernstein and Elyse Schein, *Identical Strangers: A Memoir of Twins Separated and Reunited* (New York: Random House, 2007).

14. Ibid.

15. Tim Wardle et al., *Three Identical Strangers* (Universal City, CA: Universal Pictures Home Entertainment, 2018).

16. *American Baby*, 68–77.

17. Ibid., 66.

18. Ibid., 95–96, 138–140, 243–246.

ABOUT THE AUTHOR

RUSS POMMER, a retired aviation lawyer, is a first-time novelist with a rich background. Growing up on Long Island Sound, his love of the water is deeply ingrained. A graduate of Williams College, he also holds a JD degree from the University of Pennsylvania Law School. Currently, Russ divides his time between Arlington, VA and Naples, FL. His debut novel, BIRTHRIGHT BAY, reflects his diverse interests, appealing to book groups, adoptees, nautical enthusiasts, and anyone seeking a compelling story.

Milton Keynes UK
Ingram Content Group UK Ltd.
UKHW031116261124
451585UK00004B/502

9 798990 649002